"I'm falling in l

Brody murmur

"I've got to go," Kate protested, not moving an inch. "I've got to, uh, go grocery shopping. You should see my fridge."

"I don't want to see your fridge, Katie."

"It's pathetic. All those leftovers…"

"I want to see your body…"

She swallowed hard. "Wilted lettuce…"

"I want to slowly undress you by candlelight…"

Perspiration dotted her forehead. "Some awful beef Stroganoff…"

"I want to make wild love to you, Katie."

A small pulse throbbed in her throat. Hell, her whole body was throbbing. Her insides were like marshmallows melting over a hot flame. And Brody was that flame.

"But I guess if you *really* have to go grocery shopping…"

Dear Reader

We hope you have enjoyed talented Elise Title's **The Hart Girls** trilogy, which ends this month with Kate's story. Elise had a wonderful time writing this fun mini-series about three sisters and there is more pleasure to come in Temptation from this popular author.

You should look out for Elise Title's gripping mainstream novel, *Hot Property*, which has a dramatic Hollywood background. This will be available from November 1995, published by Mira Books.

Happy reading!

The Editor
Mills & Boon Temptation
Eton House
18-24 Paradise Road
Richmond
Surrey
TW9 1SR

HEART TO HEART

BY

ELISE TITLE

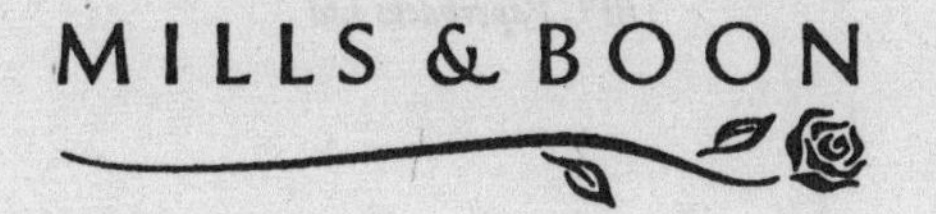

DID YOU PURCHASE THIS BOOK WITHOUT A COVER?

If you did, you should be aware it is **stolen property** as it was reported *unsold and destroyed* by a retailer. Neither the author nor the publisher has received any payment for this book.

All the characters in this book have no existence outside the imagination of the author, and have no relation whatsoever to anyone bearing the same name or names. They are not even distantly inspired by any individual known or unknown to the author, and all the incidents are pure invention.

First published in Great Britain in 1995
by Harlequin Mills & Boon Limited, Eton House, 18-24 Paradise Road, Richmond, Surrey TW9 1SR

ISBN 0 263 79453 9

21 - 9510

Printed in Great Britain by
BPC Paperbacks Ltd

Prologue

October 15

I've been thinking about this for a long time, and now that I'm fourteen (which means that in less than four years I'll be off to college, then off to find fame and fortune as a journalist), I've finally made up my mind. My mom *definitely* needs to have a man in her life. By that I mean she needs a husband—someone who'll love and cherish her for all time. (Okay, it's corny, but since this is my own personal journal that no one else on the face of this earth is ever going to read but me, I figure I can get mushy from time to time.)

My Aunt Rachel and Aunt Julie agree completely that Mom needs a man, especially now that they're both so happily married. Not that they discuss it with me, but they're always trying to fix my mom up. There were a couple of times Mom broke down and said okay.

First there was Duke. A cop friend of my Uncle Delaney's who was visiting from N.Y.C. Aunt Rachel badgered Mom and got her to go out with him. She said he even looked like Delaney—with blond hair and those great greenish gold eyes. The date was a *disaster*. (So I overheard when Mom called Aunt Rachel the next morning to give her a piece of her mind.) It seems Duke, who didn't look anything like Delaney, spent the whole evening telling Mom about one gruesome murder case after another. In vivid detail. Blood. Guts. Gore. Mom couldn't touch one piece of her rare steak. When she came home she had a terrible case of indigestion and had to dose herself with antacids.

Then there was Lester Moore, a photographer friend of Aunt Julie's. Only Aunt Julie hadn't seen him in, like, ten years. I think he must have spent most of those ten years eating. He was about Mom's height—five foot eight or so—and had to weigh close to three hundred pounds. As Mom said, this was a case where "Les was more"! We all laughed, but the fact remains, things did not work out with Lester. Not that his weight was the "big" issue. There was his ex-wife that he spent the whole evening complaining about. Mainly because she was "just too independent for her own good!" Well, since they don't come more independent than my mom, she gave good ole Les a piece of her mind. When she got home from that "date," she had a splitting headache and had to down two extra-strength aspirin.

I was beginning to despair. I mean, let's face it, there aren't that many available guys hanging around out here in dull old Pittsville—population 4,000. Even come the summer when the tourists pour into the Berkshires, they're mostly couples and families. There are a few singles' bars, but my mom would as likely be found hanging out in one of those places on the lookout for a guy as she would be found hanging out in our kitchen baking a cake. Mom's terrific and has many talents, but baking isn't one of them.

Like I said, things were looking pretty bleak. After Mom's miserable blind dates, courtesy of her two sisters, she vehemently refused to let either of them fix her up again.

And then along came Oscar. Oscar Foote. A "delightful" man Grandpa Leo and his girlfriend (soon to be wife) Mellie met on a cruise through Alaska this past summer. They raved about him to Mom practically every night for a good two weeks. A successful lawyer in his mid-forties, widowed, handsome, charming.... Well, you get the picture. Let's just say Mom was dubious—especially coming on the heels of her other two blind dates. She was also pretty cynical. Then again, Mom's pretty cynical when it comes to men—under the best of circumstances. She and my dad, as I've said lots of times in the past, didn't exactly have a great marriage. (Added note: Dad and his new wife just had their third kid. As if the twins aren't bad enough, now when I go out to Cleveland to visit them, I'm going to get stuck having to baby-sit three little monsters.)

To get back to Oscar. I don't know if it was the great selling job Grandpa Leo and Mellie did, or if they just managed to wear Mom down, but she eventually agreed to meet this "incredible" guy who, it just so happened, was planning a visit to the Berkshires to look for some investment property.

When Oscar showed up at our door one night back in late August, both Mom and I were surprised and relieved to see that he really was damn handsome. And a great dresser. He reminded me of one of those cool, sexy lawyer types from that TV show, "L.A. Law."

By Mom's fifth date with Oscar (they went out five nights in a row!) I was sure—heck, the whole family was sure—this was "the one"! You couldn't believe Mom. It was like in those romance books you read (okay, so every so often I read one or two of them; woman cannot live by biology and history textbooks alone!). Mom was floating on air, walking on cloud nine. She didn't even get on my case about folding the laundry or picking up my room. Which meant I was floating out there on cloud nine, too.

Did I have even the slightest inkling that something was wrong? I'd like to say I did because I pride myself on having this sixth sense about people (although I did think Uncle Delaney was a "hit man" when he first came to town and started making a play for Aunt Rachel), but the truth is I thought Oscar Foote was great. (Except for his name. Mom agreed, but like she said, "What's in a name?" Or was it, "A rose by any other name is still a rose"?) The point is, we couldn't find any other fault with Oscar. And like I said, I could tell Mom really was going ape for him. Not that she'd admit it outright. I'd say things to her like, "Boy, doesn't Oscar dress nice?" or, "Oscar sure is funny," and she'd sort of grunt in a way that you couldn't exactly tell whether she was agreeing or had something caught in her throat.

The way you could tell that Mom was wild for Oscar, though, was that she got herself a new hairstyle over at Carol's Cut and Curl. Not too short—just above her shoulders—but with a lot more bounce, thanks to a body wave. Aunt Rachel told her it was sexy. Even Aunt Julie who always goes to this special posh salon in Manhattan to get her hair done, had to admit that Carol did a "more-than-adequate job" (which, coming from Aunt Julie, is a major compliment). Typical of Mom, she shrugged off all the compliments. "What's the big deal?" she'd say. "It's only a haircut."

Only it wasn't "only a haircut." (Or only a body wave.) She even had Carol add a henna rinse, so now her brown hair had these real gorgeous red highlights. (The red's started to fade out now and Mom's back to basic brown. Aunt Rachel's been bugging her to at least get a trim. Mom just tells her she has no time for such nonsense. Actually, even with her hair the way it is, Mom still looks pretty darn good, even if she thinks she's "totally average." Regardless of what Mom thinks, Aunt Julie says men would find Mom attractive if she wore a ski cap on her head and a sackcloth. It's just that Mom insists she's "not interested.")

But she sure was interested in Oscar Foote for a while there, so I know that isn't really true. Right after her second date with Oscar, Mom even went out and bought herself two new dresses. Not her usual blah "working woman" dresses that she wears to the station, but these real slinky sundresses, the kind with thin little straps and real fitted at the waist. I have to tell you, my mom may be thirty-five years old, but she has a pretty good figure for her age. (Oh, and that's another thing. Mom started working out at the newly expanded health club here in Pittsville. Naturally, she claimed it had nothing to do with Oscar Foote and that it was simply to "relieve stress.")

Not that Mom's work isn't stressful. Running your own television station is no snap. Even with the help of Aunt Julie and Aunt Rachel. And right now things are really chaotic, what with her program director having just split up with his wife and taken off for Hawaii. Without even giving notice. Aunt Rachel would have helped out, but she's pregnant with her second kid and is having morning sickness, so she can't even do her own work at the station a lot of the time. And Aunt Julie's busy hosting "Pittsville Patter" with her husband, Ben Sandler, as well as taking on a daily afternoon talk show.

Oops, I'm drifting from the saga of Oscar Foote. Like I was saying, by the end of the first week, he and Mom were a "hot item." And then, one more *disaster* struck. A much bigger *disaster* than her previous ones with Duke and Lester.

What happened was, that wife of Oscar's who had (according to Oscar) died so tragically in an automobile accident a couple of years ago, "rose from the dead" and showed up right here in Pittsville about six weeks ago. With sweet, charming "widowed" Oscar's three-year-old kid in tow. Seems it had taken Mrs. Foote and the private eye she'd hired six months to track her runaway hubby down.

Not that Oscar's wife wanted him back. All she wanted was the two hundred grand or so he'd emptied from their joint bank account. About fifty thousand of which he'd just plunked down as a down payment on this great little cottage on the fanciest street in Pittsville. (From what eavesdropping I managed to do, the picture I got was that he blew most of the rest of the money, as well.) Shortly after Mrs. Foote arrived, Oscar also blew out of town. For parts unknown. I couldn't believe he had the nerve to drop Mom a note before he snuck off, telling her that she really was a great woman and if things had been different (ha!) they could have "made beautiful music together." Give me a break! I may get a little corny at times, but I've never been that bad. And even if I ever was, I certainly wouldn't put it into a letter for someone else to read.

I've got to hand it to Mom. She took it all like a trouper. I mean, the jerk deceived her and then ran out on her. I'd have been raving mad. When I wasn't locking myself in my room, crying my eyes out.

Mom can be so cool. I never once saw her shed a tear, and she didn't explode or even make one of her typically cynical remarks. In a way, that was how we all knew she was really hurting inside. If she hadn't fallen for Oscar, there's no way she wouldn't have had plenty to say about what a great big jerk he was. And she wouldn't have used the word *jerk*.

Oscar Foote! I'd like to have taken that big old "foote" of his and stuck it right down his throat.

The thing of it is, I can't stop thinking about how happy Mom was for that brief while. I don't think I've ever seen her that happy. Mom would rather be strung up by her thumbs than admit it, but I believe, deep down, she's really a romantic at heart. I bet she's secretly yearning for her knight in shining armor to come galloping into Pittsville and sweep her off her feet.

Not too likely, right?

Well, that's where you're wrong. Dead wrong.

Okay, so Brody Baker didn't come galloping into Pittsville on a white charger, but it was close. He came zooming into town on a magnificent black Harley. And talk about "knights." Brody would have fit right in at King Arthur's Round Table. Or on one of those covers of a romance novel. The minute I laid eyes on him, I knew he was the one for Mom. So did Aunt Julie and Aunt Rachel.

Now, all we have to do is convince Mom of that. . . .

1

KATE HART SAW IT as a really bad omen, the way she kept running into Brody Baker. Or, more accurately, the way he kept running into her. It all started on a Thursday morning in mid-October. She'd arrived early at WPIT to sort through more than a dozen résumés of people applying for the position of program director. Of all the applicants, only one had the right qualifications for the position and he'd been fired from his last job as the program director of a San Francisco cable station, indicating "personality differences." Kate was immediately suspicious.

Feeling depressed over the possibility of filling the position, not to mention a general malaise that she kept telling herself was a flu, she decided to take a break and go get some coffee and a sweet roll over at the Full Moon Café. While she was dating Oscar Foote, she'd given up eating fattening foods and had spent her mornings at the gym instead of a coffee shop. Now that he was out of her life—and good riddance to him, she always felt compelled to add—she could go back to indulging her sweet tooth and work off her stress on a counter stool instead of a StairMaster.

She was crossing the street, trying to decide whether or not she should interview that one potential but questionable applicant for program director, when she was nearly run down by a huge black motorcycle coming down the street. She leaped back up on the curb in the nick of time. The driver, dressed in black leather jacket and skintight jeans, squealed to a stop a few feet past her and got off the bike the way a rodeo rider might have dismounted from a bucking bronco he'd brought masterfully under control. Kate stood there fuming, arms crossed over her chest, green eyes taking on a hard, defensive edge, as she watched the motorcyclist remove his shining black helmet, shake his near-shoulder-length sandy blond hair loose and saunter toward her. In dusty, worn cowboy boots.

That very first instant she set eyes on the man, warning signs in flashing red neon went off in her head. She pegged him as brash, arrogant, inconsiderate, disgustingly self-assured, and madly in love—with himself. True, she was making a lot of assumptions about a guy she didn't know from Adam, but for the most part, her first impressions about men in the past had definitely been borne out. She'd only slipped up twice. The first time with her ex-husband, Arnie Pilcher, and recently with Oscar Foote. In both instances, she'd foolishly erred on the side of positives rather than negatives. At least with Arnie, she could blame her poor judgment on youthful inexperience. She'd been all of nineteen when she'd fallen for his phony charm and boyish appeal. She had no excuse whatsoever for having been duped by Oscar, however. She definitely should have known better. Accepting the fiasco with Oscar as a wake-up call, she came to the conclusion that if a woman wasn't careful, no matter how savvy she was about men, she could be tricked if she dropped her guard. Well, her guard was well in place as the motorcyclist ambled up to her.

"Are you okay?" The man's tone was solicitous enough, but his blue-eyed gaze held a distinct hint of amusement.

"No thanks to you," Kate retorted, but the way he was looking at her put her on edge. She impatiently pushed her hair away from her face.

He casually unzipped his black leather motorcycle jacket, revealing a black T-shirt underneath. Kate wondered if he wasn't one of those Hell's Angels. Then she asked herself what a Hell's Angel would be doing in a place like Pittsville? Stirring up trouble, that's what.

He wagged a finger at her, but his expression remained amused. No, Kate decided. Insolent. "Didn't your mother ever teach you to look both ways before you crossed the street?" he drawled.

Kate's mouth twitched in outrage. "You're trying to say that it was my fault that you nearly ran me down? Didn't your mother ever teach you that you should obey such things as speed limits?"

He glanced up and down the street. "I don't see any signs indicating the speed limit." His gaze found its way back to her and seemed perfectly happy to remain there. "Do you?"

He leaned slightly toward her. She stepped back nervously and was instantly irritated with herself. "The speed limit is thirty miles an hour in the downtown," she replied coolly.

He grinned, revealing incredibly even, white teeth. "And exactly where is 'downtown'?"

Kate's voice chilled from cool to cold. "You're standing in the middle of it."

His hands darted out toward her suddenly and Kate didn't just take another step back, she literally jumped back, afraid he was about to accost her.

"Hey, relax. I just thought maybe you wanted to make a citizen's arrest," he said, that languid smile back on his face.

Kate now saw that he was merely holding his hands out as if he wanted her to handcuff him. Not that she doubted for an instant that he was deliberately baiting her. And enjoying every moment of it.

Well, she would put a stop to that.

"Look," she said curtly. "If you're passing through, I'd suggest that you drive that bike of yours at thirty miles per hour until you're outside the town limits." With that, she stepped off the curb and started across the street.

"Hey," he called out to her, "what do you suggest if I'm not just passing through?"

Kate pretended not to hear him.

"HOW'S IT GOING?" Betty, the short, stocky fifty-year-old waitress, asked as she plucked a freshly baked pecan-and-honey sweet roll from the pastry case and set it on a plate for Kate. Betty had been a fixture at the Full Moon Café for over twenty years. Invariably, while she asked her "regulars" how things were going, she'd already formed a firm opinion about the correct answer herself.

"Fine. Just fine," Kate said, pinning on a smile. Of course, Betty and everyone else at the Full Moon—make that everyone in Pittsville—knew about Kate's brief "relationship" with Oscar Foote. At least the pitying looks had started to subside from most faces. That didn't include Betty's, however. Betty had made it clear on numerous occasions just what she thought of that "no-account bastard, Foote." And as if to rub salt on Kate's wound—although Kate knew that wasn't Betty's intent—Betty invariably added that she'd known he was a con artist the very first time she'd set eyes on him. It was "as plain as the nose job on his face."

"Margo says she hasn't seen you at the gym in weeks," Betty went on, her eyes shifting from the coffee she was pouring into a large white mug, over to Kate. "Sugar or Sweet 'n Low?"

"Sugar," Kate said a touch defensively.

Betty slid the sugar bowl and creamer over to Kate, who dropped three heaping teaspoons into her coffee, topping it off with a hefty dose of cream. After her second date with Oscar, she'd gone on a diet, deciding she should lose five pounds even though her new beau had insisted she had a perfect figure. The day after he left town, she'd bought herself a quart of Swiss chocolate almond ice cream and finished it off in one sitting. Luckily she had a fast metabolism.

Mug and plate in hand, Kate started to turn to her right, heading for one of the empty booths to avoid any more chitchat with Betty, when she collided with a man just as he was approaching the counter. Kate saw a flash of blond hair and black leather before she let out a yelp as the coffee splashed down the front of her teal-blue suit. Meanwhile the sweet roll slid off her plate and would have landed on the floor if his hand hadn't darted out to catch it.

"I was a football player in college," the man quipped, holding the sweet roll in the palm of his hand. Then, seeing that the coffee had spilled over her suit, he became solicitous. "Say, are you . . . ?"

"Don't," Kate snapped. "Don't ask. Not again."

They both reached for the napkins in the stainless-steel holder on the counter at the same time. Kate was so annoyed—she'd just gotten the suit out of the cleaners—that she literally swatted his hand away.

"Okay, okay. I'm just trying to help," he said, rubbing his hand playfully.

"I'd hate to see you in action when you weren't meaning to be *helpful*," Kate muttered, using a clump of napkins to blot the wet splotches running down both her jacket and her skirt.

"Here," Betty said, sliding a damp checkered cloth across the counter. "This will work better. Lucky," she added, "you put all that cream in so at least the coffee wasn't all that hot."

Kate exchanged the wet glob of napkins for the cloth and resumed her attack on the stains. "Oh, what's the use? I can't go around all day looking like a walking Rorschach. I'll have to run home and change."

"Have your coffee and sweet roll first," the man said. "I bet once it dries it won't be that bad." Before she could respond, he turned to Betty.

"Another coffee for my friend here and one for me. Plenty of cream in mine, too. Oh, and I'll have one of these scrumptious-looking sweet rolls, as well," he added, setting Kate's back on the plate she'd put down on the counter.

Kate snatched up her plate and shoved it into his hand. "Don't bother. You can have this one," she said icily and stormed across the coffee shop and blasted out the door.

Brody's eyes met Betty's. She grinned up at him. "Don't mind her. She's going through a tough time. This guy she was nuts over walked out on her less than two months ago."

Brody nodded sagely, tapping his index finger against his lips. "I had a feeling it was something like that."

"It's not the whole story," Betty said with a conspiratorial smile.

Brody swung his tall, lanky frame onto a stool. "Is that so?"

Betty poured him a cup of coffee, then, seeing as how the coffee shop was empty, poured one for herself and leaned toward him, resting her elbows on the counter. "It's like this. . . ."

KATE KNEW HERSELF WELL enough to know that she'd overreacted back at the café, but there was just something about how that guy kept on getting in her way that got to her. Something about the guy himself, as well. She hated cocky men. Still, she knew it wasn't only him. There were plenty of other reasons why she was so on edge lately.

Topping her list was the seemingly impossible task of finding a decent, experienced program director for WPIT. She had to face the fact that anyone who wanted to make it in television wasn't likely to see a local little UHF station in Pittsville as the place where they were going to win fame and fortune. To make matters worse, her sister Rachel, who'd been in charge of selling advertising time for all their shows, was going through horrible bouts of morning sickness and Kate had no choice but to pick up the slack. All of that on top of having to make sure the whole operation continued running smoothly. It was getting to be too much for her. Her hours at the station kept stretching in both directions. Three times this week, she'd had to leave her daughter, Skye, to manage her own breakfast and get off to school on her own. True, Skye was fourteen years old and could manage just fine, but Kate had always made a concerted effort, especially being a single parent, to be at home with her daughter until she went off to school and to be home to have dinner with her each evening. In the past couple of weeks, she'd missed at least four evening meals with Skye and felt miserable and guilty about every one she'd missed.

As if worrying about the station and about her daughter weren't enough, there was her ex-mother-in-law adding to her grief. Agnes Pilcher, a bossy know-it-all, had been the head honcho at the station before Kate and Agnes's only son—and pride and joy—had divorced. Much to Agnes's consternation, Kate had ended up with sole ownership of WPIT as part of the divorce settlement. Agnes would have liked nothing more than to buy her out; her greatest hope was that WPIT would fall enough into the red so that Kate would be forced to sell. The truth was, except for the success of "Pittsville Patter," which had been bought for syndication by a number of small-town markets, there were no other big moneymakers on the schedule. Advertising money was tight and revenues weren't what Kate had hoped they would be. If she could just nab a bright, clever program director, maybe . . .

Maybe! Maybe if she hadn't had those two "near-fatal" encounters with that motorcycle maniac, she wouldn't be in such a rotten mood right now. Or at least, not *as* rotten.

AN HOUR LATER, Kate, who had rushed back home to change into a simple gray sheath, returned to the small white Colonial building that housed WPIT. As she came in the door she wrinkled her nose. Something smelled awful.

She stepped into her sister Rachel's office, a bright, airy, pastel room whose lace-curtained front windows faced the green. Rachel was reaching for her coat as Kate walked in. A winsome beauty with a halo of auburn curls and a peaches-and-cream complexion, Rachel, at the moment, was looking decidedly green around the gills.

"I'm sorry, Kate. I just . . . can't . . ." She clutched her stomach. "The smell . . ." Even with the window open and a crisp autumn breeze blowing into the office, the strange aroma managed to permeate the room.

"What is it?" Kate asked warily.

"One of Meg's...concoctions. Don't ask me to...go into . . . detail. I've got to . . . get out of here. Sorry . . . Kate."

Kate sighed. "Don't worry. I'll man the fort."

Rachel rushed out of the office toward the exit while Kate headed straight across the hall for the studio where Meg Cromwell of WPIT's "Cooking with Meg" fame—or was it infamy?—was busy at work for her show that would be airing later that afternoon. Kate was certain that hardly anyone in the viewing audience ever replicated any of Meg's "inventive" recipes, but they loved watching her meet the challenge of topping her own weird creations week after week. Meg rarely let her audience down. Fortunately, her audience never had to smell the food she prepared.

Meg Cromwell, a diminutive woman with short, frizzy brown hair and oversize red-framed glasses that were forever sliding down the bridge of her nose, was busy chopping onions and throwing them into a large, steaming aluminum pot on the stove. When Kate walked in, the pungent aroma of garlic mixed with something sickly sweet-smelling enveloped her. Her stomach turned. What on earth could Meg be cooking?

Meg, who was just under five feet, had to stand on a footstool to work comfortably at the counter. She greeted Kate with a big smile, even though there were tears running down her face.

"It's the onions," she said cheerily, dabbing at her eyes with the heel of her hand.

"What...are you making?" Kate asked, although she wasn't so sure she wanted a detailed description, given the state of her stomach.

Meg, having finished depositing all the chopped onions into her pot, smiled brightly. "Earthy smelling, isn't it?" she said, waving her hand over the heavy steam rising from the pot, directing it toward her nose and breathing in deeply.

Kate could only guess that her resident chef's nasal passages had been desensitized after years of smelling her own cooking.

"I call it Autumn Hot Pot. It's got everything in it but the kitchen sink," Meg said with a chuckle.

Kate didn't doubt it.

"Want a sample?" Meg asked, reaching for a ladle.

"No, no," Kate said hurriedly. "I...I just...had a...big breakfast. Over at...the Full Moon," she mumbled, averting her eyes. She never had been good at lying.

Meg dipped the ladle into the pot and sampled the concoction herself. She gave a little frown, and her glasses, which had steamed up, slipped down her nose. Absently she shoved them back. "Still needs something."

"There's still the kitchen sink," Kate deadpanned.

Meg got a laugh out of that, but then she quickly returned to pondering what was missing from her Autumn Hot Pot. She snapped her fingers. "I know. I could add some TVP. To give it more texture and body."

Meg's comment reminded Kate of something quite similar that Carol over at Carol's Cut and Curl had remarked about her hair. Maybe Meg was a frustrated beautician.

"Now the question is—chunks or slices?"

Kate looked bewildered. "Chunks or slices?" she echoed. "What exactly is TVP?"

"Textured vegetable protein," Meg replied as if Kate were living in the Dark Ages not to know what the letters stood for. "Wonderful stuff. Some of the flavored varieties contain egg albumen or whey, but since this dish is strictly vegan—you know, as contrasted with lacto-vegan—we have to use the unflavored kind because there can't be any dairy products in the stew. And certainly no meat."

Kate could only nod, at a loss for words.

"I say we go with chunks," Meg said with conviction, pouring oil into a pan and setting it on a high flame. "I'll sauté them first. And, just to spice things up a bit, I think I'll toss in a little red wine. What do you think?"

Kate thought that Meg should take her pot and her TVP and deposit it in the nearest trash can, but she merely shrugged.

The studio door opened and Gus, WPIT's short, overweight stage manager, walked in and exclaimed, "Holy cow! Who forgot to throw out yesterday's garbage?"

Kate nudged Gus in the ribs. Meg, busy sautéing her chunks of TVP, shot the stage manager an icy look.

"Don't you start up again, Gus Duncan. If there's anyone around here who could do to change his diet and start eating good, healthy dishes like this, it's you."

"I'd rather die young, thank you," Gus quipped. He loved to tease Meg and she loved to scold him for not taking good care of himself. Kate, as well as everyone at the studio, believed that the pair had a long-standing crush on each other, but neither one of them would admit it.

Gus did a quick setup of the cameras, then headed back out of the studio, the door swinging closed behind him. Kate was about to follow suit, but Meg stopped her.

"You should think about your diet, too," Meg scolded Kate lightly.

Kate's hand went instinctively to her stomach, feeling for even the slightest sign of a paunch. And sorely regretting that apple pie she'd consumed after dinner the night before. Maybe it was just as well she hadn't gotten to eat that sweet roll over at the Full Moon after all.

Meg grinned. "Oh, I don't mean that kind of a diet, Kate. You have a great figure. I was talking more about nutrition," she said, stirring her sizzling high-protein meat substitute, then opening a bottle of wine.

"You're right," Kate quickly agreed, wanting to make her exit. The wafting aroma of the TVP was only making matters worse. She started to turn and head for the door, but was stopped dead in her tracks by Meg's shriek of alarm.

To her horror, when Kate spun back around, she saw flames rising from the pan on the stove. Meg, still holding the wine bottle, was so panicked she slipped off her footstool and tumbled to the floor.

"Oh, dear. My ankle. I think I twisted it," she moaned, as Kate rushed over, not knowing what to tackle first—Meg or the fire. As the flames continued shooting up from the frying pan, the stew pot began to boil over and started sizzling and sputtering. Then the smoke alarm went off.

Meg waved her off as Kate bent toward her. "I'm okay. Hurry, or the whole place will burn down!" Meg cried out frantically.

Kate grabbed for the fire extinguisher on the wall and was busy wrestling with the safety catch. "Oh, damn," she muttered. "It's jammed."

The next thing she knew she was being shoved aside. She was so startled, she stepped back, tripping right over Meg who was still sitting on the floor nursing her injured ankle. Kate landed right beside her.

Kate recognized the worn cowboy boots. Getting to her feet, she watched her "nemesis" snatch a lid off the counter and throw it over the fry pan, dousing the flames instantly. Snatching up pot holders, he removed Meg's rapidly boiling "hot pot" from the burner and turned both burners off.

He then turned to her, producing what she deemed was a totally inappropriate cocky grin. "There. Does that even the score?"

Before she could reply—just as well, since she was at a loss for a quick comeback—Gus rushed in on the noisy, chaotic scene. The fire was out, but there was still plenty of smoke. He looked over at Kate and the stranger in the biker outfit. "What happened?"

"Oh, my poor hot pot!" Meg cried, still sitting on the floor, concealed behind the counter.

"Meg?" Gus called out anxiously. "Where the hell are you?"

Kate and Brody Baker were helping Meg up when Gus came rushing around to her.

"She thinks she twisted her ankle," Kate told her worried-looking stage manager who quickly took charge of Meg, lifting her up in his arms.

"I'll drive her over to the clinic for an X ray," Gus said.

Meg, snug in Gus's embrace, didn't utter a word of protest. As he carried her out of the studio, she did, however, call back to Kate, "Don't worry. I'll get back to the studio as quickly as possible and fix my hot pot right up."

Kate, distracted by this latest surprise encounter with her "Hell's Angel"—he did look alarmingly dangerous—almost said okay to Meg, but managed to come to her senses before the cook was carried off. One Autumn Hot Pot was one too many.

"I won't hear of it, Meg," Kate said. "You go right home after you're checked out and take it easy. We'll just do a rerun."

It wasn't until Gus had carried Meg out of the studio and the door had closed behind them, that Kate noticed the tear in the hem of her dress. She must have gotten the heel of her pump caught in it when she fell over Meg. She scowled. Was practically *pushed* over Meg, was more like it. She was itching to give the push*er* a piece of her mind, holding him responsible now for messing up not one outfit but two. And it wasn't even noon yet. As angry at him as she was, however, she couldn't very well ignore the fact that he'd prevented the studio—hell, maybe even the whole building—from burning down.

The smoke having cleared, he stood there, leaning against the counter, casually studying her as if she were put there for his leisurely inspection. Refusing to let him unnerve her, she stared defiantly back at him.

"What are you doing here, anyway?" she demanded.

"Saving your beautiful neck," he replied, with that same cocky grin of his that set her teeth grating—and, much to her chagrin, set her heart thumping. However irritating she found his personality, she couldn't deny that he was dramatic looking with those wild, windblown blond locks, those Paul Newman blue eyes, that rugged, square jaw, and that long, lanky cowboy build.

"Aren't you even going to say thank-you?" he asked. "I know you were brought up to have good manners, so I'll have to assume you've just forgotten them in the *heat* of things."

"And just how do you know how I was brought up, if I might ask?" she asked archly, instantly chastising herself for sounding like a prig. Really, the man was impossible. He simply brought out the worst in her.

The cocky grin shifted to a mischievous smile. "Oh, Betty and I had a nice little chat about this and that over at the Full Moon. Terrific sweet rolls they've got over there. You really should have stayed, Kate."

Usually a pro at hiding her feelings, Kate felt her face redden just imagining what Betty might have told this perfect stranger about her. Why could no one in Pittsville ever mind their own business?

Kate cleared her throat, determined not to give the man the satisfaction of embarrassing her even more. "Thanks for putting out the fire. I . . . I do appreciate it, but I really have to clean up this mess and set up a rerun and . . . I've got a million other things to do, so . . ."

"I'm a pretty good cook," Brody said casually. "How about if I clean up and pinch-hit for your TV chef?"

Kate looked at the man as if he were crazy.

He grinned. "What? You don't think I can cook? Do you like chicken?"

"Look, Mr.—"

"Pork? Veal? Filet of sole? I make a mean sole Amandine."

"I don't like fish."

"Okay, chicken. How about *suprêmes de volaille sauté andalouse?*"

He spoke French like he was born to it. Despite herself, Kate was impressed. She wondered if maybe he was French-Canadian. Then she got annoyed at herself for wondering anything about this man she was trying to get rid of.

"Really," she said, "I don't have time—"

"Exactly. So, I'll clean up this mess." He peered into the pot. "What is this concoction, anyway?"

"Don't ask."

He laughed. "Okay, so I'll clean up, run down to the supermarket—"

"What supermarket?"

"Whatever goes for a supermarket here in Pittsville."

"There's only Cobb's Grocery Store. It carries strictly the basics. If you want anything fancy you have to drive over to the Grand Market at the shopping plaza in Louden." Why was she even bothering to tell him this?

"The dish sounds fancy, but all it calls for is chicken, flour, oil, butter, scallions, tomatoes, a pinch of tarragon, parsley, dry wine and a splash or two of cognac, of course." He was rummaging through one of the cupboards on the set as he spoke and came up with a bottle of olive oil and a tin of flour.

"Cognac. Of course," Kate said dryly, her cooking expertise limited to such specialties as spaghetti with meat sauce—more often than not, store-bought meat sauce from Cobbs.

He was examining the burned pan. "I'll give this a good scrubbing. I should be able to save it. I assume you don't want me to save what's in the pot."

"God, no."

They both laughed. Kate stopped first, feeling like a traitor.

"It's not that I...don't appreciate your...offer," she said. "It's just that it would be a lot easier to just plug in a rerun. I'm sure you have better things to do than . . . this."

"Not really. I've got nothing on my schedule."

"Well, I have plenty on mine."

He plucked a rubber band out of his biker jacket, pulled his hair back from his face and fashioned a ponytail at the nape of his neck. "There. Now I won't get any hairs in the dish."

"Listen—"

He cut her off. "I know what's getting to you."

It wasn't *what*. It was *who*. "I really don't think you do." Or so she hoped.

"You think I'm gonna hit you up for a paycheck."

"No. I mean, if you did think I was going to pay you, you could forget it."

"Then it's the chicken. You don't like chicken."

"I like chicken just fine. It's just—"

"Great. So, I'll make the dish for the show and then afterward, we can eat it. Your place or mine."

"Yours?"

"Great."

"No," she said hurriedly. "That wasn't a statement. It was a question."

"Run it by me again."

"You have a place in Pittsville? You live here?"

"Yep."

She eyed him suspiciously. "I've never seen you before. And, if you do live here, how come you didn't know the speed limit?"

He set the burned pan in the sink and was filling it up with water. "I just moved in yesterday. Rented a little bungalow over on Kenyon Street from a real nice lady by the name of Louisa Carpenter. Do you know her?"

Did she know her? Kate knew every living, breathing person in Pittsville. She happened to know Louisa Carpenter especially well. She'd gone to school with her. She'd been to all three of Louisa's weddings. And listened to her lament over all three of her divorces. That the divorcée had rented the bungalow on her property a stone's throw from her own house to this long-haired "biker dude," as her daughter, Skye, would have called him, was going to set the whole town buzzing. Not that gossip had ever stopped Louisa. Nor, judging from the look of him, did Kate think it would stop Louisa Carpenter's new tenant.

On top of this, Louisa's house was only a few short blocks away from Kate's. That made her and this biker practically neighbors. Well, she might not have anything to say about them living near each other, but she definitely had the last word about them working together at her station. Even if it was only for one cooking show.

She drew her shoulders back, placed her hands on her hips. "I'm sorry," she said firmly, "but I can't have you cook the chicken."

He looked up from the burned pan he was scrubbing. "Okay, I'll cook something else. How about—?"

"No. I don't want you to cook anything. I don't want you to clean up. I don't want . . ." She was about to say she didn't want to have anything more to do with the man, but she felt she couldn't be that rude since he had come to her rescue, despite the mayhem he had already caused her that day. And, much to her consternation, was managing to continue to cause.

"Okay, okay. I'll just finish this pan—"

"That won't be necessary," Kate interrupted, eager for him to leave. The man made her exceedingly nervous. What was he doing here in Pittsville, anyway? She knew if she asked him, it would only delay his departure. Anyway, she told herself she didn't care why he was here; only that he disappear.

When she saw that he was still scrubbing the pan, she got miffed and tried to grab it out of his hands. The next instant, her dress was covered in soapy water.

She opened her mouth to speak, but she was so angry the words wouldn't come. He held up his hands in surrender.

"Out," she finally managed to say in a low, hoarse voice.

He smiled sheepishly, wiped his hands on his jeans, and with what Kate viewed as a decidedly macho swagger, ambled across the studio toward the door. When he got there, he turned back to her, the smile on his face no longer sheepish, but downright sexy. "I'm going to make you that *suprêmes de volaille sauté andalouse* one of these nights, Kate Hart. And you're gonna go wild for the taste."

Kate turned scarlet as he made his dramatic exit.

2

AT A LITTLE AFTER FOUR that afternoon, Kate sat at her desk, palms propping up her chin, once again going over the résumé of her one potential candidate for program director. She was particularly unsettled by the fact that the applicant, a thirty-seven-year-old single male, hadn't gone into any of the details of the "personality differences" between himself and his employer—a *female* employer, she noted—that had led to his being fired from his previous job. Prior to that position, he'd held several other similar jobs in radio-and-television programming, all out on the West Coast. He didn't, however, indicate whether he'd quit or been fired from those jobs, as well. All in all, his résumé raised a lot of questions.

There was a rap on her door.

"Yes?" Kate called out.

Perky, red-haired Kelly Nelson, who had been Kate's secretary since graduating from high school that past June—and was still the makeup girl for the local talent that appeared on WPIT—popped her head in her boss's office.

"Line one," Kelly said, one plucked dark brown eyebrow raised.

"Who?" Kate asked warily, recognizing that arched brow as a sign of trouble.

"Your ex-mother-in-law."

Trouble with a capital *T.* "Oh great. That's all I need. You don't have any idea what she wants?" Not that it mattered. Kate knew whatever it was, it wouldn't be anything good.

"I think it's about Meg's show this afternoon. She said something about..." Kelly paused, pursing her lips and squinting à la Agnes Pilcher. "Isn't Meg Cromwell starting to repeat herself?" She mimicked Agnes's scratchy voice to perfection. "I'm sure she cooked that very same roast lamb with prunes and apricots last year."

"I suppose I'll have to tell her it was a rerun," Kate said wearily. "I'm sure she'll have any number of suggestions about what I should have done instead of repeating an old show. That'll be her lead-in to criticize everything else she feels is wrong with how I run this station."

Kate sighed as she reluctantly reached for the phone. Before she lifted the receiver she hesitated, her hand wavering right over that résumé she'd been agonizing over. So she had a lot of questions about the applicant. The least she could do was listen to his answers.

"Kelly," she said, picking up the résumé, "give this guy a call. Ask him if he'd be willing to fly in from San Francisco for an interview sometime next week. Monday, if possible. If I don't find a program director soon, I'm going to be hearing from Agnes daily."

As it was, Kate got a running critique on her performance as head of WPIT from her ex-mother-in-law several times a week. Which was several times more than she would have liked. Maybe if Agnes had had any real talent herself for running the station when she'd been in charge, Kate wouldn't have felt so bitter and frustrated by her constant criticism. Agnes totally lacked creativity and hated to take any risks. Furthermore, her ideas and methods for running the operation had been outdated even ten years back. And worst of all, she was incapable of relegating any authority, wanting to be in charge of everything. And everyone. While Arnie had ostensibly owned the station, he'd been quite content to let his mother run things. He'd basically been allergic to responsibility. Besides, it had given him a lot of spare time for extracurricular activities!

Kelly crossed the room and took the résumé from Kate's hand. "We could get an unlisted number," she whispered, as Kate lifted the receiver to her ear.

Kate grinned. "That's an idea," she murmured to Kelly.

"What idea?" Agnes demanded with that same scratchy tone in her voice that Kelly had imitated so expertly a few moments earlier.

"I was just finishing up something with Kelly," Kate responded, hearing the edginess in her voice. And realizing Agnes would, too.

"No reason to be snippy," her ex-mother-in-law chided.

Kate smiled ruefully.

"By Kelly, I take it you mean that so-called secretary of yours?" Agnes inquired archly, knowing full well that was exactly whom Kate meant.

"Really, Kate," she went on. "The girl doesn't even know how to answer a phone properly. I'm quite sure she was chewing gum when I spoke to her. It makes a terrible impression. If you really felt a secretary was warranted, you should have at least hired someone from a secretarial college. Granted, you'd have to pay them a higher salary, which might be a problem for you, but as I always said to Arnie, you get what you pay for. Arnie had the good sense to take my advice."

Kate had to bite back a sharp laugh. Oh, her ex-husband, Arnie, had taken his mother's advice, all right. He'd hired himself a gorgeous twenty-three-year-old brunette with a figure to rival Madonna's right out of the Fletcher Secretarial School. Sue Ellen Redfield. Only thing was, Arnie's secretary had a talent for more than shorthand and answering the telephone. Kate was pretty sure that Sue Ellen wasn't the first woman Arnie'd had an affair with during their marriage. She was just the first one Kate had found out about. A little matter of her husband coming home late from work several times a week, his shirt smelling of Sue Ellen's inimitable scent—eau de Home Wrecker.

When she'd confronted Arnie directly one winter night nearly six years back, he'd handed her a double whammy. Not only did he openly admit that he and Sue Ellen were indeed having an affair, but that he wanted to marry her. To add insult to injury, he'd actually had the nerve to tell her that while he still loved her and Skye, he was "in love" with Sue Ellen, and surely she would understand he had to follow his heart. *What* heart? Kate had ruefully thought at the time. When she wasn't crying her eyes out behind closed doors. It was the last time she'd cried over any man. They weren't worth it.

"Kate? Kate, are you listening to me? Have you heard a word I've been saying?" Agnes's sharp voice intruded on her ruminations.

Kate gave her head a little shake to clear out the cobwebs. Dwelling on the past wasn't usually her thing. And her relationship with Arnie was definitely a thing of the past. "You were saying you aren't impressed with Kelly," she said in a tired monotone.

"I said that over a minute ago. I must say, Kate, you can't very well run an entire station and be daydreaming all the time. I was talking about Meg's show this afternoon. I am quite sure she cooked that—"

Kate cut her off. "It was a rerun, Agnes. Meg had a little. . .mishap and couldn't do the show at the last minute."

"A mishap? What kind of a mishap? And how did it happen?"

"It was nothing serious. She just sprained her ankle." Kate wasn't about to go into the details of Meg's "accident," although she knew that by the end of the day, the story would have spread through town of how Meg had almost burned the studio down while preparing her Autumn Hot Pot. Agnes would be quick to phone her back and get her two cents in about what she would no doubt term the "catastrophe" that would somehow have been yet one more indication to Agnes of her ex-daughter-in-law's incompetence.

Although Kate knew she was only biding her time, she simply didn't have the strength to cope with her ex-mother-in-law at the moment. Too many things had already gone wrong that day and she was afraid she might end up saying something to Agnes in the heat of anger that she'd regret later. Regardless of what she thought of Agnes Pilcher, Kate knew it was best to keep those thoughts to herself. Anyway, when Agnes wasn't being such a pain in the neck, Kate actually felt sorry for her, believing that deep down Agnes was simply a lonely, insecure woman afraid of growing old.

"You might have at least picked a better rerun, Kate. I thought that lamb-and-prune dish was particularly unappealing and my guess is, so did most of our viewers."

Kate was quick to pick up the "our" viewers. Agnes absolutely refused to accept that she no longer had any role to play at WPIT—never mind that she was no longer running the show.

"I really have to go, Agnes. I have to be at the rehearsal for this week's 'Patter.'"

"Then let me get right to the point, Kate."

And here Kate had naively thought Agnes had already made her point. She tried to steel herself for what was to come, knowing whatever it was, it wasn't going to improve her mood any.

"You are in desperate need of a program director," Agnes declared. "Not to toot my own horn or anything, but I doubt that there's anyone you're going to find who's more qualified than I am for the position. For just about any position at WPIT, for that matter. When Arnie was in charge, he was only too happy to trust my judgment regarding just about every aspect of the operation."

Kate smirked. Agnes didn't *toot* her horn. She *blasted* it!

"Certainly not that I need the work. Or the headaches. Arnie's father, may God rest his soul, made sure I was well looked after. It's simply that WPIT is almost like my...baby, and I can't turn my back when my baby needs me. I am well aware, Kate, that we don't always see eye-to-eye on things, but no one should be too proud to admit when she needs help."

Help? That was a laugh. Kate knew that if ever Agnes managed to get her foot back in the door of WPIT, she'd be shoving Kate right out of it.

"That's very...kind of you to offer, Agnes. The thing is, I've already found someone. A very experienced fellow from a top cable station out in San Francisco. He's flying in next week and if he looks as good in person as he does on paper..." Kate shut her eyes. Maybe he really would look better than she thought. One thing was for sure, however he looked, he was going to look better than Agnes Pilcher.

Kelly came back into the office just as Kate was hanging up the phone.

"Did you reach him?" Kate asked immediately.

"No. Some woman answered, but she said she'd get word to him and have him call back."

"She didn't happen to say who she was?"

Kelly smiled impishly. "Maybe it's his sister."

"BET YOU FORGOT TO bring home the pizza," Skye called out from the top of the stairs as Kate walked into the house that evening—empty-handed.

"Damn, I knew there was something I was forgetting," Kate mumbled as her daughter came bounding down the steps. "Sorry. It totally slipped my mind. What little mind I have left."

Skye gave her mother a sympathetic pat on the shoulder. "How about if we go out for pizza instead? I finished all my homework."

"I don't know, Skye. I'm kind of beat. It's been...one of those days."

"Come on, Mom. Just think, if we go out for pizza you won't have to slave over a hot stove. Well...over a microwave. And anyway, have you checked the freezer lately? We're down to one turkey pot pie and a box of fruit pops."

Kate eyed her daughter with faint amusement, struck by how pretty and grown-up she was looking these days. No more braids, for one thing. Now Skye wore her thick brown hair in a sophisticated pageboy cut. And even in baggy clothes, Kate could see her daughter was developing a very cute figure. "This wouldn't have anything to do with Robby Mitchell working over at Village Pizza now, would it?"

"Oh, please, Mom. Robby is a jerk. He's totally immature. And just because he got on varsity soccer this year, he thinks he's hot—" Skye grinned. "Hot stuff."

Kate laughed. "And you want me to believe you and every other girl at Pittsville High don't think he's hot . . . stuff?"

"Every other girl, maybe. But give me credit for having better sense."

Kate gave her daughter a hug. "Never too young to have good sense when it comes to men," she said dryly. It wasn't Oscar Foote or even her ex-husband that flashed into Kate's mind. It was that brash and cocky biker. She realized then that she didn't even know his name. Not that it mattered, she hurriedly told herself. She already knew enough about him to know she wanted absolutely nothing further to do with him.

THERE WERE ONLY a couple of vacant tables left at Village Pizza—the only pizza parlor in Pittsville—when Kate and Skye arrived shortly before eight that evening. Kate started to steer Skye over toward an empty table in the back when she spotted her sister Julie and Julie's husband, Ben, sitting at a table for four over by the window facing onto the street. They made quite a handsome pair, the two of them, each with their short blond hair; Julie oozing class and sophistication, Ben radiating classic anchorman good looks. Julie spotted her sister and niece at the same time and motioned them over.

"We just ordered a large pizza with sausage," Julie said as Skye and Kate slid into the empty seats. "Why not share it with us and then we can all splurge on cannoli for dessert?"

"Sounds good to me," Kate said. She felt she was entitled to a fattening dessert, having passed on her sweet roll that morning, thanks to— No, she wasn't going to think about that impossible man again. She turned to her daughter. "What do you say, Skye? Sausage pizza and cannoli?"

Skye, however, wasn't listening. She was staring intently out the window. Kate figured it was probably Robby coming in from a pizza delivery, but when she followed her daughter's gaze she let out a little involuntary gasp. It wasn't Robby who had drawn Skye's attention. It was that damn biker. He had just pulled his gleaming black Harley up to the curb a little ways from the pizza parlor. It made Kate feel a little weird inside, the way he kept popping up wherever she happened to be—like she'd created some kind of magnetic force field or something.

"Wow!" Skye exclaimed, her eyes widening, her cheeks flushed as she watched Brody Baker hang his helmet on his handlebar and then smooth his wild blond locks away from his face. "Now there's a dude who puts Fabio to shame."

"Who's Fabio?" Ben asked, not up on the dashing male model who'd come to fame by posing for a huge number of historical-romance novel covers.

"Forget Fabio. Who's the guy with the bike?" Julie mused.

"Whoever he is," Kate said tartly, "he's impossible."

All eyes at the table turned to her. Kate realized her faux pas immediately. Why hadn't she just pretended not to know him from Adam? Not that she really did know him from Adam. Not that she wanted to.

"You know him, Mom?" Skye asked with astonishment.

"No." Now she was lying to her own daughter. "Not really. Not exactly." She smoothed a red paper napkin on her lap. Where was that pizza already?

"Come on, Kate," Julie urged, ever the nosy journalist. "Out with it. Who is that gorgeous hunk of manhood? What's he doing here in Pittsville? And how did you get to meet him?"

"Hey—" Ben eyed his wife with a teasing smile as he swung an arm possessively around her shoulder "—you mean to tell me you go for that type?"

"What type?" Julie quipped. "Tall, blond, gorgeous, sexy?"

"I'm tall, blond, gorgeous and sexy," Ben drawled.

Julie pecked her husband on the cheek. "Why do you think I married you, silly?" Her gaze fell on Kate. "I may have landed my tall, blond, gorgeous, sexy dreamboat, but my sister's still available," she added, her eyes sparkling.

"Please," Kate said, stretching out the word. "He's not my type."

Julie grinned. "Honey, he's any-woman-in-her-right-mind's type."

"He is cool, Mom," Skye seconded. "Hey, I think he's coming in here. He is."

"Let's ask him to join us," Julie said. "Skye, go find another chair. We can all squeeze in a little. It'll be cozy."

Kate's hand shot out and she grabbed her daughter's arm before she'd risen an inch from her seat. "Don't you move. I most definitely do not want that . . . that man to join us. Don't you even look his way. That goes for the rest of you, too."

Julie opened her mouth to protest, but Ben gave his wife a faint shake of the head.

Julie sighed. "Okay. Okay."

As the door to the pizza shop opened, Kate snatched one of the almost-never-used menus that was wedged between the saltshaker and the stainless-steel napkin holder and popped it in front of her face. Ben, Julie and Skye all shared very curious looks.

"Relax, Mom. He's just picking a pizza up for take-out," Skye whispered to the other side of the menu.

Probably bringing it back to his bungalow to share with his landlady, Kate figured. Not that it mattered one iota to her who he shared his pizza—or anything else—with.

He left just as their pizza arrived. Kate set her menu down. Just a moment or two too soon. There was a rap on the other side of the window. Instinctively, Kate looked over. It was him. He wore a grin that could have melted a polar ice cap, but Kate's expression remained frozen.

She instantly turned away from him, pretending to ignore the sea of stares at her table.

"Where is our pizza, anyway?" Kate muttered.

ON FRIDAY MORNING as Kate arrived at WPIT, she was disconcerted, to say the least, to see what was becoming an all-too-familiar-looking black Harley parked at the curb right in front of the station. Really, she thought as she started up the path to the front door, this was too much.

Kelly was already at her desk when Kate walked inside.

"He's here," Kelly said brightly.

"Oh, he is, is he?" Kate replied, her green eyes glinting.

"I told him he could wait in your office."

Kate drew her shoulders back and marched over to her door. She threw it open, strode into her office and shut the door firmly behind her. Kate's office was quite spacious, but little attention had been paid to decor. It was strictly functional, with gray industrial carpeting, a large metal desk, a sturdy oak swivel chair she'd picked up at an auction and a threadbare tweed sofa that her father had pawned off on her when he'd redecorated.

Kate found him sitting on her sofa, looking completely at home, one leg stretched out in front of him, the other bent at the knee, the heel of his boot resting on the edge of her pine coffee table, arms languidly outstretched across the back cushions. His black biker jacket was tossed carelessly over a nearby chair. He'd exchanged his black T-shirt for a faded red chambray shirt with the sleeves rolled up to reveal muscular forearms, and substituted black jeans for blue jeans, the black pair equally worn and equally tight. The scruffy boots, one of which remained displayed on her albeit scratched-up, wobbly coffee table, were the same.

For all her irritation, the sight of this blond Adonis set off little charges inside her. What had Julie said last night about him being any-woman-in-her-right-mind's type? That should have exempted her. She certainly hadn't been feeling like she was in her right mind lately.

Then, how to explain the suddenly escalated pulse rate, the strange sensation in her belly, the sweaty palms, the disturbing but undeniable tug of those bluer-than-blue eyes . . . ?

Luckily, Kate had recently installed a fail-safe built-in alarm system for just such emergencies as she was currently experiencing. If a man turned her on, it sent off an instant warning that he was definitely no man for her.

"Just what are you doing here?" she demanded.

"I believe you sent for me," he said laconically, his blue eyes flicking over her, taking in the trim red blazer that she was wearing over a turtleneck sweater and a slim-fitting short black skirt. "Say, I like that outfit better than the other two you had on yesterday."

Kate ignored the compliment although she couldn't ignore the way his continued appreciative study of her made her feel. "I sent for you?" He was a liar to boot.

The Paul Newman eyes sparkled. "I know. You're perturbed that I'm early."

"I am not perturbed," she countered, planning to go on to tell him that she was extremely annoyed. And what the hell did he mean, he was "early"?

He cut her off before she could ask.

"Good. Being flexible is a very admirable quality in a boss."

Kate did a classic double take. "A what? Did you say a boss? Oh, come on, pal. If you want to do a television cooking show that badly, why don't you go talk with Julia Child in Boston? She's getting on in years. Maybe she's looking for a replacement."

He tapped his temple with his index finger, grinning at her at the same time. "Think about it a minute, Kate. You know who I am."

"I know you're becoming a public nuisance."

"Baker? Brody Baker?"

No, Kate thought. It wasn't possible.

His grin broadened. "Starting to ring a bell? Dawn starting to light?"

"No." This time she said it aloud. "No. You can't be."

He sat forward, flicking his blond hair back from his shoulders, a languid smile on his face. "Annie called me from San Francisco last night and told me you wanted me to come in on Monday for an interview. Since I was already here and I got the impression from Annie that you were eager to see me, I figured why wait till Monday."

Kate felt utterly daunted by his revelation. She still could not fully accept that he was Brody Baker, the applicant for the job of program director that she had, indeed, sent for. "What are you doing here?"

"Didn't we just clarify that?" he asked with a teasing grin.

"I mean..." What *did* she mean? She'd suddenly lost her train of thought. If only he'd stop smiling at her like that; stop looking at her like that; stop giving her the feeling that he was having such a good time at her expense.

"I had another job interview in Boston this past Monday. On Tuesday, I bought myself a bike and decided to drive on over here to Pittsville and take a look around. I liked what I saw. I grew up in a small town in Ohio. Nice living in a place where you know everyone."

"So you knew who I was the whole time," Kate said angrily. "And you deliberately hid who you were from me."

"Whoa. Did you once take the time to ask me who I was? I had the distinct feeling you didn't want to know."

"You're right," she said, peering down at him.

He stood so that now he had the advantage. "Come on, Kate. Admit it. You need me."

"What? You're crazy. You're absolutely not what I need."

"Then why'd you send for me? Why'd Annie get the feeling the job was in the bag?"

No doubt it was Kelly's doing. Kate decided she'd have to have a little talk with her secretary.

"Well, Annie's wrong. Whoever Annie is. The job's *not* in the bag," Kate said archly.

"Annie's my—"

"I'm not interested."

He grinned but he didn't say anything.

"And frankly, Mr. Baker—"

"Brody."

"Mr. Brody—"

"No. Brody Baker."

"Will you please stop confusing me?"

"It's just that if I'm going to be calling you Kate, you, as my boss, can't very well go around calling me Mr. Baker."

"I am not your boss. I have no intention of being your boss."

"According to Mellie Pilcher you do."

Kate blinked rapidly. "When did you meet Mellie?"

"I gotta tell you, Kate, Mellie and your dad make a damn good-looking couple. The wedding they're planning sounds like a real humdinger."

Kate sat down on the sofa. She needed to. "You met my father, too?"

"Great guy. We all ended up having breakfast together over at the Full Moon. You should have stopped by. The sweet rolls were even better this morning. Fresh out of the oven. Betty was gonna wrap one up for me to bring you, but I told her I didn't want you to think I was trying to bribe you."

He sat down beside her. "Anyway, Mellie was telling me how her sister Agnes called her last night and told her you were hiring this terrific program director from San Francisco. . . ."

"I never told Agnes you were terrific." Kate frowned. Or had she? She couldn't remember what she'd said now. She couldn't think straight.

"Now, don't start worrying that I'm gonna try to hit you up for a big salary."

Kate laughed sharply. "Believe me, it's far from big. In case you haven't heard—but then I imagine you've heard just about everything there is to hear—I run this operation on a very tight budget. Revenues are down, several local advertisers have had to pull out over the past couple of months, we've had to invest in a new TelePrompTer, our sync generator is in desperate need of updating—" She stopped as she saw him smiling at her. "What's so amusing?"

He leaned a little closer, his blue eyes sparkling with amusement—and something else that Kate couldn't quite read. Or didn't want to. "You know," he murmured, "you're actually quite beautiful when you talk fiscal."

3

KATE WAS ABOUT TO launch into a diatribe of why he was absolutely the wrong man for the job when her office door opened.

Kate's sister Rachel stopped halfway through the door, her gaze falling on the sexy, long-haired biker.

"Oh, hi again," Rachel said warmly.

Kate stared at her sister in disbelief. "Again?"

"Oh," Brody said laconically, "didn't I mention that Rachel and I met over at Cobb's Grocery Store yesterday afternoon?"

"So, how did your chicken *andalouse* come out?" Rachel asked, ignoring Kate.

"Great," Brody said enthusiastically. "In fact, I was just about to tell your sister what she missed."

He shifted his gaze to Kate. "You can pick up that rain check. Got plenty left over. It's even more tasty the second day," he added, those blue eyes flashing.

Kate wore a sardonic smile. "If your chicken dish was so great, how come you were picking up a pizza last night?"

"I wasn't picking it up for me. My landlady's car was on the fritz and so she asked me if I wouldn't mind—"

"Village Pizza makes deliveries," Kate said, cutting him off.

"Really, now? I guess that must have slipped Louisa's mind," Brody drawled.

Kate was quick to pick up on Brody's use of his landlady's first name.

Rachel laughed. "Nothing slips Louisa's mind, Brody. I bet when you brought that pizza back she invited you in to sample some of her . . . slices," she quipped saucily.

Exactly what Kate was thinking but was not about to verbalize. The pair was welcome to become eating buddies or anything else, as far as she was concerned.

Brody grinned at Rachel. "She did at that."

Kate compressed her lips. Really, that Louisa Carpenter was so pathetically obvious. No doubt just the kind of woman a man like Brody Baker would go for.

"'Course, I had to turn her down," Brody murmured, his eyes now fixed on Kate. "I was plum full from my own dinner. And anyway, I wanted to turn in nice and early, knowing I'd be coming in for this interview first thing this morning and wanting to look all bright-eyed and bushy-tailed."

Rachel grinned. "You look at least that, Brody. Doesn't he, Kate?"

Kate felt the color creeping up her neck. She was glad she was wearing a turtleneck sweater. "Rachel, was there something you wanted?"

Rachel seemed thrown by the question. "Wanted? Oh, yes," she said after a couple of moments. "I had this great idea. I wanted to run it by you before I talked to Julie and Ben about it. I was thinking it would be great to have Brody here on their next 'Patter' show. They could introduce WPIT's new program director and get his—"

Kate sprang up from her seat, palms flat on her desk. "Wait a minute. Just wait one little minute, here. Who said anything about Brody here being my new program director?" she demanded.

Rachel stared at her sister, nonplused. "Well...pretty much everyone, Kate. Mellie and Dad. Julie. Agnes."

Kate's hands went to her hips. "Well, in case everyone's forgotten, I'm running the show. I do the hiring and firing. I make the decisions about who is and who isn't—"

Kelly popped her head in the door. "Your favorite critic on line one."

Kate's heart sank. "Agnes?"

Kelly nodded, her gaze shifting to Brody and then back to her boss. "Should I tell her you're in an important meeting with your new program director?"

AFTER HER OFFICE cleared and Kate was once again left alone with Brody, she felt like she'd been jammed right into a corner.

Brody rose from the couch, pulled up one the chairs in front of her desk and spun it around so he sat down on it backward, his arms folded across the back of it as he stared across at her.

He smiled sympathetically. "Will it help any if I tell you I didn't plan it this way?"

Kate stared back at him. "No."

"I really am a damn good program director, Kate. I've got some great ideas—"

"Why'd you get fired from your last job?"

He hesitated. "Like I said. Personality differences."

"That's not saying very much," she countered. After a pause, she added, "Your boss was a woman."

He rested his chin on his crossed arms. His blue eyes were suddenly very serious. "Yes, she was a woman. A very conservative woman. She vetoed some of my most creative ideas because she didn't want to rock the boat. She didn't want to take chances. She lacked vision."

"And that's the whole story?" Kate prompted.

Brody lifted his head and grinned. "So, it's the whole story you want, is it?"

"What I want is to understand why you were fired," she said stiffly. "Just cut to the chase, Mr. Baker."

"The chase." He eyed her thoughtfully. "The chase is...she wanted us to have more than a...professional relationship. I didn't. Once she realized I wasn't going to change my mind, she found having me around . . . irritating."

Kate didn't say a word. She didn't have to.

Brody broke into a grin. "I do grow on some people."

She looked dubious. "Really?"

"Sue Morgan wasn't my type. There was no chemistry."

"And if there had been?"

Brody took his time answering, his gaze remaining fixed on Kate. "I don't honestly know."

Kate narrowed her eyes. "Well, I happen to feel very strongly that people who are involved in a . . . professional relationship should never get involved in . . . in any other kind of relationship."

"Not even a friendship? I got the feeling you were pretty friendly with your chef, your stage manager. . . ."

"That isn't what I meant and you know it," she said sharply.

A faint smile played on Brody's lips. "What about your sister Julie and Ben? Didn't things start out strictly professional with them? And now they're working together as a happily married couple. I'd call that *intimate*. Wouldn't you?"

Kate squirmed. "That was an . . . exception."

He grinned. "That was chemistry."

"I am *not* my sister. Nor am I the least bit interested in . . . chemistry."

"I can completely understand that, Kate."

"Oh, you can, can you?" she retorted defensively.

"You're still licking your wounds."

She stared at him, dumbfounded. "I'm still . . . what?"

"If you don't mind my telling you, Kate, you deserve a lot better than that creep of a con man, Oscar Foote."

She felt heat flare in her cheeks. For a woman who rarely blushed, she was certainly making up for lost time around Brody Baker.

She sat up even straighter in her chair, tossed her head back and glared at him. "First of all, I do mind you telling me. And second of all, just because you picked up a few tidbits of gossip in town, don't make the mistake of believing you know anything about me, Mr. Baker. Because you don't know a thing. And I'd just as soon keep it that way."

She cleared her throat, desperately trying to reclaim some semblance of sorely absent professionalism. "Anyway, I'm the one who's conducting this interview. If anyone needs knowing about in this office, it's you."

"All right," Brody said calmly. "Let's talk about me, then. What do you want to know?"

"For starters, why do you want this job? This is a long way from San Francisco. And didn't you say you had a job interview in Boston the other day? Boston certainly seems more up your alley than . . . Pittsville. Or didn't they want you?"

"They had some stipulations that just didn't sit right with me."

Kate arched a brow. "Now why doesn't that surprise me?"

A mischievous smile tilted the corner of his sexy mouth. "They wanted me to get myself a nice blue suit, cut my golden locks, ditch the boots." He lifted a boot-clad foot up to the edge of her desk. "These boots and me, we've been through a lot together. Got real sentimental value."

"Well, I'm not interested in appearances. I'm interested in—"

"What about you, Kate?" he asked, cutting her off. "You the sentimental type?"

"Hardly."

He grinned.

"What? You don't believe me? I suppose it was something Betty said. Or my dad. Or Mellie. Or one of my sisters."

"They didn't have to say anything, Kate," he replied, the blue eyes glinting.

For all her efforts to the contrary, Kate found herself flushing again. *Damn the man.*

"I'm gonna be real straight with you, Kate. What I was talking about before—chemistry? Well, I felt it the moment I laid eyes on you."

"You mean the moment you almost ran me down," she countered, trying desperately to ignore the way his outrageously flirtatious remark made her pulse speed up.

"What if I tell you I'll obey the speed limit from now on with the same sincerity that I obey my heart?"

"You really are incredible."

"Now that's the nicest thing you've ever said about me, Kate."

"I didn't mean it as a compliment. Do you honestly think I'm so naive, so pathetic, so...so small-town, that I would actually buy a cornball line like you just tossed? Do you honestly think this is the way to win a job here?"

"First of all, I believe you're anything but naive or pathetic. I think you're a smart, savvy, dynamite-looking woman. Even if you are small-town—which, I feel, is definitely in your favor. I see you as a woman with roots, values, a sense of community. I bet you even volunteer at the hospital whenever you get a spare moment." He grinned. "Fact is, I know you do. Your dad mentioned that auction you held up at the pediatric unit just last month."

Kate sighed. Had her entire family made her life an open book to this stranger?

"Second of all," Brody continued, "none of what I have to say is a line. I'm just stating facts and feelings. I believe in putting my cards—or should I say my heart?—on the table."

He paused before going on. "But putting my heart aside for a moment, Kate, I want this job because I think you are a woman with vision. A woman with passion who'd like to see your station become something special. And I want to assure you I'm going to be the best damn program director you've ever been lucky enough to lay your hands on." A sly grin flashed on his face. "Figuratively speaking, naturally."

"You make a...a blatant pass at me, toss off one...one innuendo after another and you seriously think I'm going to hire you? I may be desperate, Mr. Baker..."

"Now come on, Kate. I'm being straight with you. Why not be straight with me?"

"Meaning?"

"You *are* desperate, Kate. Don't forget now, you've got that ex-mother-in-law of yours. . . ."

It was no surprise to Kate at this point that he knew all about Agnes. Still, she wasn't going to allow Brody Baker or anyone else to influence her decision making.

"Agnes Pilcher isn't going to push me around," Kate said adamantly. "And neither are you. Everyone around here seems to be forgetting I'm running the show. I do the hiring. I make the decisions."

Brody swung his lanky frame off the chair and perched himself on the corner of her desk. "I've got some great ideas, Kate."

"I'm sure you do," she said dryly.

He placed his hand dramatically on his chest. "Okay, so I confessed you made my heart speed up when I first laid eyes on you. Now, I could have kept that a secret, but like I said, I believe in being out-front with people. Especially the people I plan to be involved with. But separate from how you make my heart beat, Kate, I like the whole setup here. I like the town. The hills. The dales. The people. Especially the people. They're warm and friendly—"

"Not all of them," Kate interjected pointedly.

Brody grinned. "Some just take a little longer than others to warm up to me."

Removing his hand from his chest, he slipped it into his jeans pocket and pulled out a couple of sheets of folded paper that were stapled together. He unfolded and extended the papers across the desk toward Kate.

"Have a look at this," he said.

Kate regarded the papers suspiciously.

"Don't worry. They're not declarations of love or anything. Just some program ideas I jotted down that I think might bring in more viewers and therefore more advertisers and finally more revenue. You don't like what you see, I'll walk on out of here and that'll be that."

Kate continued to stare at the papers Brody was holding out for her, making no move to take them from him.

"Unless the real issue here is not how attracted I am to you, but how attracted you are to me?"

"That has absolutely nothing to do with it," Kate said firmly.

Brody's blue eyes sparkled with amusement. "So you are attracted to me."

"I am most certainly, most absolutely *not* attracted to you."

"One or the other would have been sufficient."

"One or the other what?" she demanded.

"Either the 'certainly' or the 'absolutely.' Now, the fact that you felt you needed to use both, seems to me like a bit of overkill on the protestations. Could be open to some interpretation."

"This is the most insane, ridiculous job interview I have ever conducted," she muttered.

Brody smiled. "It's one I'm never going to forget, either."

She still didn't take the papers from his outstretched hand, so he simply set them down in front of her. Then he rose and ambled across the room toward the door.

When he got there he glanced over his shoulder at her. "I'll give you a few minutes. You let Kelly know when you want me to come back in. Or if you just want me to head straight out the front door."

His hand reached for the knob, but before he turned it, he looked back at her once again. "One thing, though. I'm not gonna give up the boots. And the last time I wore a blue suit was at my sister Annie's wedding and that was close to ten years ago. I just seem to think better in casual attire. As for the hair, well, that's negotiable. Anything but a crew cut. Man, I'd scare myself off in a crew cut."

After Brody walked out the door, the one thing that stuck in Kate's mind was . . . *at my sister Annie's wedding.*

Annie. Wasn't that the name of the woman who'd answered Brody's phone back in San Francisco?

She lifted up the papers he'd left behind, a faint smile on her face. As soon as she realized the smile was there, however, she immediately erased it.

No. Absolutely no. She was not going to let that irascible charmer get to her. No way . . .

Then she started reading.

October 24

Boy, was Mom in one lousy mood when she got home from work today. When I asked her what was wrong she muttered something under her breath. I didn't catch it at first, but then it hit me. *Brody.* She'd mumbled "Brody." Hmm. This is getting interesting. Especially as word has already spread through town that Mom hired Brody Baker as WPIT's newest program director this morning. Is she having second thoughts already? Hope not. I think he's totally neat.

October 30

We went over to Aunt Julie and Uncle Ben's house for dinner. I love their place. It's one of those cute white-shingled Cape Cod cottages, but Aunt Julie had the whole downstairs gutted so it looks real modern inside, with skylights and neat paintings and these cool columns separating the dining room and living room. We had take-out Chinese. The whole clan was there. Aunt Rachel and Uncle Delaney with Samantha, who's definitely the most adorable baby that ever existed. (I'm not biased even if she is my niece.) Grandpa Leo and Mellie were there, too.

Okay, so we're all sitting around the big round dining room table, which is strewn with all these little white cartons. Everyone's digging in, so there's not too much talking except for stuff like, "Where's the dumplings?" and, "Pass the soy sauce." Aunt Rachel's heaping her plate with spare ribs, chicken fingers, fried rice (but what the heck, she's eating for two). Then Aunt Julie reaches for the container of fast-disappearing fried wontons. There's only one left. She glances over at my mom, but sort of asks in general, "Does anyone want this last fried wonton?" Now the fried wontons are Mom's favorite (which, naturally, we all know), and she hasn't taken a single one, but she shakes her head.

Everyone stops grabbing and eating and looks over at her. I've just bitten into my egg roll and I hold it in my mouth for a couple of seconds, not even chewing.

Mom gives us all one of her typical "Mom" looks. "What? Isn't a person allowed not to want a fried wonton? Is it a crime? Did some law get passed about having to eat at least one fried wonton?"

Grandpa Leo, who was sitting next to Mom, patted her shoulder. "Now, don't go getting your dander up, girl." (Grandpa Leo really does talk like that. I think it's kind of cute.) "Nobody here's going to make you eat a fried wonton if you don't want to eat a fried wonton."

I couldn't help it. I started to laugh. Aunt Julie, who was sitting to my right, nudged me in the ribs. It didn't help. I still broke up. And as soon as I began laughing, Aunt Rachel started to laugh. Mellie kind of tittered softly. The men all grinned. Aunt Julie was the last holdout, and then she couldn't keep it back.

Well, actually, Mom was the last holdout. She sat there, poker-faced. And like she absolutely didn't know what was so funny. Only she did, and we all knew she did.

So, I just said it. Right there at the table with everyone but Mom laughing. I said straight-out, "I think Brody's totally awesome and I'm really glad he got the job."

Everyone else at the table agreed with me. Everyone, that is, except for Mom. She didn't crack so much as a smile. Which is really kind of weird, considering she was the one who hired Brody. Sort of. Like she said, after everyone finished grinning and nodding their heads, "He's on probation."

The way she said it, it was like poor Brody had committed a crime or something. And the message was clear that if he didn't watch his step, Mom was going to "lock him up and throw away the key."

I always thought I had Mom figured out, but she really had me puzzled. She was acting like Brody Baker was put here on this earth—or at least put here in Pittsville—to make her life miserable. So, why did she hire him?

When I was in the kitchen after dinner, helping Aunt Julie wash up the dishes, I asked her what she thought. She gave me this knowing grin. "Your mom's finally met her match," she told me with glee.

"You mean you think Mom and Brody really. . ."

I didn't even get to finish before Aunt Julie was nodding away, her eyes sparkling.

"But she acts like she hates him," I said. And then I grinned. Reading all those romance novels has not been wasted on me. "O-o-oh, I get it."

Aunt Julie gave me a little hug, but then her face got real serious. Like something was worrying her. And then she proved it by saying, "There'll be problems, though."

"What kind of problems?" I asked, curious as all get-out.

She wasn't really listening. "One thing's for sure," she says. "If this gets as serious as I think it's going to get and they end up tying the knot, Agnes Pilcher will certainly be one happy woman."

My eyes opened wide as saucers—okay, maybe not that wide. "Tie the knot? You mean. . .get married? You really think Mom and Brody. . .? But they've only known each other a little over a week. And every night Mom gets home from work, she mumbles something about how impossible he is."

I was so astonished by the first part of Aunt Julie's remark, I almost missed the second part. Wait a sec. What did Aunt Julie mean about my Grandma Agnes being one happy woman? Why would she be happy if Mom got married again?

I asked Aunt Julie and she dropped the bomb. She told me that if Mom remarries, she loses WPIT. Seems Dad gave Mom the station instead of a monthly alimony check. It also seems "alimony" stops once Mom's no longer single. She gets married and the ownership of the station goes back to my dad. And since my dad always let Grandma Agnes run the station in the past, now that he's living thousands of miles away, Aunt Julie's sure he'd be perfectly happy to let her take charge again. It would be the end for Mom. And Aunt Julie and Aunt Rachel, as well. Even if my grandmother wanted to keep them all on, I don't think there's a chance in the universe that any of them would agree to work for her.

I started throwing questions at Aunt Julie—first on my list being why didn't Mom ever tell me about the alimony situation—but she didn't get to answer any of my questions because just then Mom came in and said she had a headache and wanted to go home. She caught our dubious looks and immediately said, "It was the MSG they put in the Chinese food. I always get headaches from MSG."

Only I happen to know for a fact that our restaurant doesn't use MSG. They have a big announcement about it right on the bottom of their menus. I decided not to mention that, though, and we went home.

So, here I am at nine-thirty at night with plenty to think about. Is my mom really falling in love with Brody Baker? Is Brody Baker really falling in love with my mom? Sure, you read about it all the time in romance books, but can these things truly happen this fast in real life?

Brody Baker as Mom's husband? As my stepdad? He's certainly worlds apart from my real dad. He's like...so cool. Brody, that is. My dad is strictly straight-arrow—button-down shirts, chino pants and blue blazer, haircut razor short. Just thinking of my dad in a black leather jacket riding a motorcycle... Well, I can't even imagine such a sight. My dad drives a station wagon. With those fake wooden panels. When he isn't wearing his blue blazer, he's wears cardigan sweaters. Like the ones Mister Rogers wears on that kids' show on TV. Come to think of it, my dad looks a little bit like Mister Rogers.

One thing's for sure. No one's ever going to compare Brody Baker to Mister Rogers. So what? What's wrong with having a stepdad who's drop-dead gorgeous? Like my mother would say, Is it a crime? Is there a law against it? I mean, Brody shouldn't be penalized for looking the way he looks. It doesn't mean he isn't a kind and caring man. I'm willing to keep an open mind. What about Mom, though?

Would Mom really give up WPIT for Brody? For any man? Or would she sacrifice love for her career? Or for her sisters?

I know Aunt Julie and Aunt Rachel would encourage Mom to marry Brody if he really ever did ask her. They'd tell her to put her own happiness first.

Hold on. It just hit me. Mom and my two aunts wouldn't be the only ones out of a job. Brody would probably be out of a job, too.

God, this is awful. This is unfair. This is a *disaster!*

No, there's got to be a way for Mom to keep the station and have true love. There's just got to be. I've sure got my work cut out for me.

4

As soon as Kate walked into the station the next morning she was greeted by the blaring, heart-wrenching voice of a high soprano echoing down the entire corridor. The walls were practically vibrating. Her brother-in-law, Ben, came out of the fortunately soundproofed studio where he had just delivered the local morning news.

"What is that?" she asked him incredulously.

"*Madam Butterfly,* I believe," Ben said. "But I'm not the opera buff."

"Who is?"

Ben grinned. "Your new pal, Brody."

Kate felt all of her muscles stiffen as she gave her brother-in-law a sharp look. "He's not my *pal*. He's my employee."

Ben's grin followed her as she strode off down the hall toward Brody's office, determined to set a few ground rules with her new employee.

Brody's office—what had been an oversize pantry when the building had been a private home at the turn of the century—was the last room on the right at the end of the hall. Kate walked in without knocking. No point, since the music was on so loud he wouldn't have heard her even if she had knocked.

The tenor had joined the soprano for a duet as Kate stood just inside the door. Brody was at his desk, busily writing away. He must have sensed her presence, though, because he did look up after a few seconds. She opened her mouth to speak, but he held his hand up for her to remain silent.

"This is my favorite part," he said, closing his eyes.

Kate strode over to the portable stereo sitting on top of the built-in oak pantry shelves that still covered the length of one sidewall.

The shelves, empty the week before, were already cluttered with papers, manuals, books and tapes. The whitewashed walls were plastered with an eclectic mix of posters—everything from an Andy Warhol soup can to a Degas ballerina. There was even a small Navajo rug on the floor. Brody had wasted no time settling in. Kate reflected that he was certainly good at that as she pressed the Off button on the compact black stereo right in the middle of Brody's "favorite part."

Brody opened his eyes and squinted in her direction. "You don't like opera?"

"I don't like not being able to hear myself think." Kate found herself using much the same tone of voice that she used with Skye when she played her music too loud at home.

Brody's response, however, was unlike her daughter's breezy, somewhat sheepish, "Sorry, Mom." He leaned back in his swivel chair and gave her one of those piercingly assessing looks of his that made her instantly self-conscious.

"So what is it you're trying to hear yourself think about?" he asked nonchalantly, smoothing an errant strand of hair back from his face. He had pulled his hair back into a leather thong at the nape of his neck, which gave him a pirate look.

"That isn't the point," Kate said archly.

"It isn't?"

"No," she said sharply.

"What *is* the point, exactly?" he asked. His tone might have been innocent but Kate caught the faint smile. He was baiting her again, and she simply wouldn't stand for it.

"The point is—" Her mind went suddenly blank. What *was* the point? She glared at him. This was all his fault. Just look at the man. Sitting there so smug and self-confident. Like he had the whole world in the palm of his hand. Or, at least her, anyway.

"See what I mean? That damn music—" She threw her hands up in the air in frustration.

"Music's supposed to soothe the soul, Kate."

He rose from his chair. Kate instinctively took a step back. Then, as he started in her direction, another step. She seemed to be always in a state of retreat around Brody Baker.

He had to have noticed, but at least he didn't smile. He walked over to the built-in shelves, a couple of feet away from Kate. He lifted up a handful of cassette tapes that were piled next to the stereo and began shuffling through them. "How about jazz? Or classical?"

Kate made no response, her expression cool and guarded.

"Top forties?"

She made an involuntary face.

He laughed. "Good. Because I don't have any top forties. Not my thing, either. See, we share something in common."

She almost smiled, but caught herself in time. Not fast enough, however, to prevent a sigh from escaping.

"You need to relax a little, Kate. Now that I'm on board—"

"This isn't going to work," she said, cutting him off. "It just isn't." The words had been on the tip of her tongue all week. Whatever talents he might have as a program director, Kate simply found the man irritating. Unnerving. Distracting. No matter how cool and *professional* she behaved toward him, he seemed to get the misguided message that she was *attracted* to him. Okay, so the man did have a certain sexual appeal. But he wasn't her type at all. Not at all.

Brody folded his arms across his broad chest. Although he wasn't wearing anything resembling a blue suit, he had forsaken his T-shirt and jeans for a well-worn pale blue work shirt, which he wore with the sleeves rolled up, and a pair of slim-fitting black corduroy slacks. And still those black leather cowboy boots.

Does he wear those boots to bed? The instant that question popped into Kate's head she felt her cheeks flush. What was she thinking? What did it matter to her what he did or didn't wear to bed?

Does he wear anything? An image of Brody, stark naked, flashed into her mind. It only lasted a couple of seconds but the effect it had on her was truly alarming. Her whole body flooded with heat.

Oh God, Kate thought, shutting her eyes. *I'm losing my mind.*

"Why don't you tell me what's really bugging you, Kate?"

She shot Brody an anxious look, afraid she'd been transparent, and expecting to see at least the hint of a smirk on his face. To her surprise, he was regarding her with an utterly serious expression. Ironically, that only served to increase her discomfort. How could she possibly tell him what was really bugging her? She wasn't even sure herself.

Okay, so she had a pretty good idea. All the more reason to keep her mouth shut. She told herself Brody was like one of those twenty-four-hour viruses. They hit you completely unawares, knocked you for a loop and then, thankfully, were gone a day later and you were back to your normal self again. Kate was desperate to get back to her *normal self*.

The silence filled the room. Brody was still waiting patiently for an answer from her. So she gave him one that was certainly true if not her most pressing concern at the moment.

"Our styles. They're completely different, Brody."

"In what way?"

She rolled her eyes. "Isn't it obvious?"

"Well now, Kate," Brody drawled, "what's obvious to you and what's obvious to me may be two different things altogether. That's why it's so important for two people who are involved with each other to communicate their feelings."

"We're not 'involved' with each other. And I thought men didn't like to . . . talk about this sort of stuff," she mumbled.

"I'm not like other men, Kate."

She was beginning to believe him. Only it wasn't going in his favor. For all her negative feelings about "other" men, at least they were predictable.

Brody stepped a little closer to her. "If you give it a chance, maybe you'd discover that our styles—however different you might think they are—just might complement each other."

"I . . . doubt that," she said, averting her gaze to the Navajo rug on the floor and shifting her weight from one foot to the other.

"Man, I hate those bastards," Brody muttered.

His remark caught Kate completely unawares. Par for the course. "What bastards?"

"All those guys who did a number on you and made you so bitter."

Kate flushed. "They didn't. I'm . . . not. There weren't . . . that many. Anyway, that has absolutely nothing to do with . . ."

He took another step closer to her. Kate found she couldn't finish the sentence. All of her energies were directed at fighting her almost-overpowering impulse to back away from him again.

"Give me an inch, Kate," he murmured.

Oh sure, Kate thought. Give a man like Brody Baker an inch and he'd take a foot. *Her* foot, at that!

"We're not all bastards, Kate. You're way too young to close yourself off. You've got a lot to offer a man."

His tone was soft and suggestive and for a moment she got lost in it. This conversation was not going as planned. She'd come in there merely to chew him out for blasting his music. How had it come to this? Kate had no idea. All she knew was that she absolutely had to pull herself together.

"You just don't get it, Brody. I need a program director, not a . . . a man."

He gave a rich, full laugh. "Not much I can do about my sex."

"Damn it, Brody. You know what I mean. And it's precisely the fact that you choose to . . . to do what you do . . . that makes it clear as day that we are not going to be able to work together."

There was absolute silence as they eyed each other.

"You canning me, Kate?"

She *wanted* to can him. She wanted him to pack up his stereo and all of his tapes and the rest of his paraphernalia and walk out the door. And keep on walking. Out of the building. Out of Pittsville. Out of her life.

So why couldn't she get a simple *yes* out of her mouth? Somehow that tiny little word had gotten stuck in her throat. Somehow, all she seemed to be able to concentrate on were Brody Baker's compelling, bluer-than-blue eyes and those finely chiseled lips.

His lips parted slightly. So did hers, although she didn't mean for them to.

No, no. That wasn't true. She couldn't very well say yes if her lips were sealed. And she wanted to say yes. Absolutely. Definitely.

Yes to what, though? She'd lost her train of thought.

His head tilted to the right and began to dip toward her. For some reason she couldn't fathom, she found herself tilting her head to the left.

Just say it. Just say yes and it'll be settled.

"Yes." The word came out as an urgent whisper. An instant before their lips met.

It wasn't only the exquisite sensation of Brody's mouth pressing lightly on hers, it was the way he brushed her cheek with his hand in the tenderest of gestures at the same time, that sent Kate reeling. She'd expected rough, macho, take-what-you-want lust from Brody Baker, which, heaven help her, she was just weak enough at that moment to have responded to—and then would have regretted afterward for all time. Instead, he completely threw her by being so gentle and not taking advantage of what he had to know was his advantage.

The kiss, his feathery touch, was over almost before it had begun. Almost as if it had been her imagination. Only, what Kate was feeling wasn't her imagination. Something stirred inside her that had been lying dormant for years. She couldn't really identify what it was, exactly, but it made her pulse race, her palms sweat, her head swim.

Brody was still very close. His warm breath fanned her even-warmer face.

That danger sign in her mind kept flashing. If she didn't turn away now, she'd be a goner.

She turned away.

Good girl. She was proud of herself.

Her pride lasted all of five seconds, before she spun back around and threw herself into Brody Baker's arms with such force she knocked him against the On button of the stereo. As their lips met for the second time, the room was flooded with a hauntingly passionate duet from Puccini's star-crossed lovers.

All of Kate's sense of self-preservation—never mind constraint and dignity—vanished as their mouths connected this time around. It was her tongue that darted past Brody's warm lips to tangle with his. She circled her arms around his neck. She pressed her body into his, weak with desire as she practically clung to him for support.

Brody was more than willing to provide that support. He wound his arms around her waist, slipping his hands under her sweater to feel her bare skin. She moaned at the touch.

The music was soaring and they were wrapped in each other's arms, kissing wildly, when Kate heard a faint, "Oh . . . excuse me," coming from the direction of the door.

Even so, it took her a few seconds to register that someone had actually entered the office. When it did finally hit home, Kate's hands flew up to Brody's chest and she shoved herself away from him as if she'd been scorched.

Humiliated, her cheeks blazing, she spun around to face a most embarrassed-looking Harry Beckman, owner of Beckman Hardware, which was around the corner from the station on Elm Street. Harry, a heavy-set man with thinning hair and wire-rimmed glasses, was blushing furiously.

What was Harry doing here? What could she say to the man? How could she explain to him what he'd witnessed when she couldn't even explain it to herself? Besides which, Kate knew that no explanation was going to keep this shameful incident from spreading through town like wildfire. Harry Beckman, whom Kate had known practically her whole life, was up there with the best of them when it came to being one of the town's gossips.

"Kate," Harry mumbled in greeting.

Kate could only manage a faint nod, averting her gaze.

Unlike Harry and Kate, Brody seemed remarkably unruffled by the intrusion. He calmly turned off the stereo and beamed a friendly smile at the pudgy-faced, middle-aged interloper.

"Hi ya there, Harry."

The hardware-store owner cleared his throat. "Sorry about . . ." He paused, cleared his throat again. "I guess . . . what with the music . . . and *all*, you didn't . . .

hear me knock," he muttered, shuffling his feet and running his hands nervously down his plaid flannel shirt before shoving them into the pockets of his khaki work pants.

"No problem, Harry," Brody said amiably. "Kate and I were just . . ."

Kate glared at Brody. "I was just leaving."

"No, don't leave," Brody said, his fingers circling her wrist as she turned to make a quick exit. "You should be part of this meeting."

Kate couldn't believe how calm and unperturbed Brody appeared. Had the man no sense of . . . of decorum? Of professionalism?

Professionalism? Ha! That was a laugh, considering she was the one who had practically thrown herself at him.

Practically? There was no "practically" about it. She had behaved abominably, wantonly. Not to mention, utterly uncharacteristically. Kate was filled with self-loathing. All she wanted to do was get away.

She tried to tug her arm free from Brody's firm grasp. "I really . . . have . . . a lot of . . . work. And . . . things to . . . do. I don't . . . have time." The words came out disjointed and she felt like a babbling idiot.

"First you have to meet Mr. Fix-It," Brody said effusively, refusing to let go of her.

It was yet another of Brody's curveballs that found Kate responding in astonishment, "Mr. Who?"

Harry smiled sheepishly. "I don't know, Brody. I've never really seen myself as a . . . TV personality."

Kate stared at Brody, dazed. "A TV personality? Harry?" Then, realizing how unintentionally insulting that must have sounded to the hardware-store owner, she hurriedly apologized to him.

"No offense taken, Kate," Harry said assuringly, smoothing back his thinning brown hair. "I told Brody when he dropped into the store yesterday afternoon and we got to chatting about this idea of his, that it was kind of a crazy notion."

"Exactly what is 'this idea'?" Kate asked Brody, her tone sharp.

Brody smiled affably. "Look, Kate, we've got five late-afternoon/early-evening slots that we're presently filling with tired old reruns. My idea is to start filling those slots with live, local shows. Look at the success you've had with 'Pittsville Patter.' Not that every new show I come up with might be suitable for syndication, but we could breathe a little new life into the station and increase revenues dramatically with local advertisers."

Brody's words flew by Kate in a jumbled rush. She tried to concentrate, but her traitorous mind kept slipping back to that passionate kiss they'd just shared. How could Brody switch gears so quickly? Her answer was that he probably did it all the time; that what had happened hadn't meant much of anything to him. The man was a hustler, a snake-oil salesman, and she'd gone and blithely bought out his whole stock of phony wares. What an idiot, what a jerk, she'd been.

Brody was still hawking away. "The minute Harry and I got to talking yesterday, the idea hit me right in the face. Did you know that this man is a positive wealth of information about everything having to do with building and household-repair stuff, Kate?"

Kate continued chastising herself mightily.

"So here's what I'm thinking. I want to put Harry on right after 'Cooking with Cromwell,'" Brody continued, his deep-timbred voice awash with enthusiasm. "A half-hour spot where we'd have Mr. Fix-It give our viewers helpful tips about repairing leaky faucets, putting down linoleum, weather-stripping doors and windows—you name it."

"And don't forget your other idea," Harry prompted, clearly not as reluctant to become a television celebrity as he had first appeared.

Brody winked. "Right you are, Harry," he said, and turned again to Kate who, at this point, was maybe catching every other word. "I thought we could have folks write in and ask specific questions for Mr. Fix-It to answer. That might be a good way to wrap up the show. Say, a final ten-minute spot. What do you think, Kate?"

What did she think? The nerve of the man asking her a question like that at a time like this.

"I think," she said tightly, "we should talk about this later. And," she added in the same stiff tone, brushing past Harry as she headed for the door, "other *things*, as well."

"Great," Brody called brightly after her. "I'll take you to lunch."

"No," she called back.

He chuckled. "Okay, you can take me."

BRODY SHOWED UP AT the door to Kate's office at noon on the button. He rubbed his palms together and smiled engagingly at her.

"Ready? I don't know about you, but I'm starving. I hear they make a mean meat loaf at the Full Moon. On second thought, maybe we should go somewhere else. Someplace less . . . public. We could drive out of town, find a nice little out-of-the-way dining spot. I've got an extra helmet if you want to go on the bike. Or if you'd rather we take your car..."

Kate, seated behind her desk, folded her arms across her chest. "You think this is all one big joke, don't you?"

He stepped inside, shut the door and leaned against it. "Would it make you feel better if we went Dutch?"

She opened her mouth to say something biting, but instead a sigh escaped from her throat. "I don't know what came over me before." She stared down at her desk, shaking her head. "I really don't. I never behave...like that. I think I must be...coming down with something. And your office...it was so warm. No, it wasn't the office. I'm not sick. I have absolutely no excuse. It was...completely inappropriate. My behavior was...utterly... unprofessional."

She was so absorbed in chastising herself and trying to make sense out of what seemed so completely crazy to her that she didn't notice Brody cross the room. When she looked up, she was startled to find him right beside her, his hand lifting her chin so that her eyes were forced to confront his.

Only she couldn't make him out clearly. For some strange reason, his face was a hazy blur. She thought her eyesight was suddenly failing her until it dawned on her that her eyes had filled with tears.

"Don't cry, Kate," Brody murmured. "We'll figure it out."

"No," she muttered, shoving his hand away. "I don't want to figure it out. I just want to...forget it ever happened."

"Okay," he said gently, wiping the tears from her cheeks with the tips of his fingers.

Again she swiped at his hand. "Just like that? You think it's that easy? Well, maybe it's easy for you—"

"Whoa. I didn't say anything about wanting to forget it ever happened, Kate. Personally, I'm going to treasure that moment forever."

Kate's tears dried up. "How many times have you used that line before?"

"It isn't a line. I think you know that. And I think that's really what's bugging you. You want me to be like all those other jerks in your life, but I'm not."

"So, what kind of a jerk are you?"

There was a moment of silence and then, in unison, they both broke out laughing. Kate stopped first.

"This isn't funny, Brody. It really isn't."

"Come on," he said, sobering up a little. "Let's go eat."

Kate made no move to rise. Instead, she reached for a sheet of paper on her desk—a letter that she'd been composing all morning. She extended the paper out to Brody.

"Here." Her expression was completely serious now.

"What is it?" he asked cautiously.

"It's a...request for your...resignation." She hadn't been able to pink-slip him. It would have meant putting all the blame on Brody for what had happened. And, as much as she would have liked to, Kate couldn't absolve herself of a good part of the blame. The simple truth was that she had *wanted* to kiss him.

And now she wanted him to have the good grace to quit.

Brody's hands remained at his sides as he stared, not at the letter, but at Kate. "You want me to resign?"

"Please take the paper, Brody." Even she could hear the note of pleading in her voice.

Obligingly, he took it from her hand. He didn't even glance at it, however, before crumpling it and shooting it over toward her wastepaper basket by the door. He landed a perfect shot.

KATE SAT THERE, scanning the faces of the other diners, as she tried to figure out how she'd ended up at Giorgio's Italian Villa on the outskirts of Pittsville sharing a meal and a bottle of Chianti with the man she had that very morning canned, kissed, then asked to resign his post as program director at WPIT.

"More wine?" Brody asked as he lifted the wicker-based bottle from the table. At the same instant he started to top off her glass, Kate's hand shot out over the rim. The wine inadvertently splashed on her hand.

"Sorry," Brody said.

"No, you're not," she snapped, refusing the red paper napkin he offered, snatching up her own from her lap to dab the splattered wine off her hand.

Brody produced one of his damnable smiles. "I gather we're not talking wine, here."

She eyed him defiantly. "Well, are you sorry?" she demanded.

"No."

"I knew that's what you were going to say."

"So why did you ask?"

"This conversation is ridiculous. Every conversation we have is ridiculous. Is this—" she paused to wave her hand around "—par for the course for you, Baker? Do you reduce all women to babbling idiots?"

"You're anything but a babbling idiot, Kate," Brody said, reaching across the table and taking hold of her hands even as she tried to draw them away.

"What am I, then?"

A beguiling smile curved his lips. "What are you?" He observed her thoughtfully. "You're bright, lovely, feisty—"

"I'm your boss."

His smile deepened. "I won't hold that against you."

"Can't you ever be serious, Brody?"

His smile vanished and his gaze became so intense that Kate's breath caught in her throat. "If I get too serious, I'll scare the dickens out of you, Kate. And you're scared enough, as it is."

"Scared? Of you? That's patently ridiculous."

"I bet you never were much of a liar."

"I am not lying."

"Hey, don't sweat it. It's one of the reasons I'm crazy about you."

"You are not crazy about me, Brody," she scolded him.

His smile was unexpectedly disarming. "Yes, I am, Kate."

"You don't even know me. You don't know anything about me." She flushed. Thanks to Pittsville's "loose lips," he knew far more about her than she cared for him to know.

A trim, young blond-haired waitress arrived to clear off the luncheon plates. Brody had finished off his lasagna, but Kate had hardly touched her pasta marinara.

"Do you want me to wrap this up for you?" the waitress asked her as she scooped up the plate of spaghetti.

Kate shook her head. She had no appetite. She doubted if she'd ever have an appetite again.

"How about you, hon?" the waitress asked, flashing a provocative smile at Brody. "You could heat it up for your dinner."

"I would, but I've got a dinner date tonight."

At Brody's mention of a dinner date, Kate felt an involuntary flash of jealousy. Who was he going to be dining with tonight? He was probably being flooded with dinner invitations from every eligible woman in Pittsville. Kate's bet was on Brody's landlady, Louisa Carpenter.

"Go on and ask me," Brody said, as the waitress walked off.

Brody's voice quickly drew Kate from her ruminations. "Ask you what?" she asked with sitcom nonchalance.

He grinned at her. "You're as transparent as glass, Katie."

"No one calls me Katie," she snapped.

"Good."

5

KATE STARED AT HER sister Rachel, aghast. "What do you mean you invited him to dinner?"

"What do you mean, what do I mean?" Rachel countered blandly.

"Don't pretend you don't know what happened today."

"A lot of things happened today, Kate," Rachel responded, a faint smile playing on her lips as she shuffled through some papers on her desk, then checked her watch. "Almost five o'clock. Time to get home and put the roast up."

Kate sank into a nearby chair and dropped her head in her hands. "I really do think I'm coming down with something."

"I'll agree with you there," Rachel teased, a little laugh escaping. Kate lifted her head and glared at her sister.

Rachel was immediately contrite. She came around her desk and put a hand on her sister's shoulder.

"What's so awful, Kate? So you and Brody kissed. It was *only* a kiss, right?"

"Of course, it was *only* a kiss," Kate retorted. "What did you hear it was?"

"Take it easy. You know how these things get... exaggerated."

Kate dropped her head back in her hands. "Oh, this is awful. I have never been so embarrassed, so humiliated, so—"

"Excited?"

Kate's head popped up. "Rachel!"

Rachel leaned against her desk and regarded her oldest sister with a mix of sympathy and frustration. "What's so terrible about admitting that Brody Baker turns you on? Come on, Kate, we'd all be worried about you if he didn't."

"I don't want to be 'turned on.' Especially not by a man who turns me *off*."

"Baloney."

"I asked him to resign today."

"And?" Rachel prompted.

"He . . . ignored me. The man simply refuses to . . . to take me seriously. He just goes about his merry way—"

"I think his 'Mr. Fix-It' show's terrific," Rachel interrupted. "And I've got to tell you, Delaney's sort of intrigued about this new idea of Brody's."

Kate stared at her sister. "What new idea?"

"That's why Brody's coming over for dinner tonight. To go over the details with Delaney. Say, why don't you come over, too, Kate? I'm making a leg of lamb and you love lamb."

"Rachel, what exactly is this idea of Brody's?"

"Hasn't he told you?" Rachel looked uncomfortable. Obviously he hadn't told Kate. "Well, maybe he wants to see if he can get a commitment from Delaney first."

"Rachel, what is it?"

"It's no big deal, really. Just a spot on the local news with Delaney taking calls."

Kate blinked several times. "Taking calls? What kind of calls?"

"You know. About . . . crime."

Kate narrowed her gaze. "Tell me if I've missed something, but last I heard, Pittsville wasn't exactly picked as the crime center of New York State. What are they going to cover? Some kid's bike getting swiped from the schoolyard? Somebody getting a jaywalking ticket crossing Main Street? Raccoons breaking into the grocery store?"

Rachel shrugged. "Come on, Kate. The people of Pittsville are as concerned about crime as everyone else. Actually, there have been several bikes stolen in the past few months. And an attempted break-in or two. And what with Delaney being Pittsville's chief of police, well, he could advise people on how to secure their homes against intruders, the best locks for bikes, ways to settle disputes without anyone ending up getting hurt. Remember when Cy Tilton and Darryl Hutchins got into that brouhaha over a dumb football game over at the high school. Hutch ended up in the hospital."

"Really, Rachel. He was treated for a black eye."

"Still, it was no way to resolve a problem."

"I don't know about that," Kate said sardonically. The idea of socking someone—namely Brody Baker—in the eye sounded quite enticing to her at the moment.

"And what with Delaney having been with the N.Y.P.D.," Rachel said, bypassing Kate's remark, "people could ask him questions about his experiences as an undercover cop, as well. Brody thought it would jazz up the local news. You said yourself before Brody came on board that viewership was down considerably, especially for the six o'clock and eleven o'clock spots. Everyone's watching reruns of 'Beverly Hillbillies' and 'Cheers,' or turning to cable. We've lost a number of local sponsors, and you know yourself that we might have to pull one, maybe both of those spots, if we don't do something to spark more viewer, and therefore more sponsor interest. Brody definitely thinks, with this added segment, more people would tune in. I think he's right. So does Julie . . ."

"Oh, so Julie knows, too. And Ben. And Dad and Mellie. Naturally, 'Mr. Fix-It' knows. And Betty over at the Full Moon. Let's see. Am I leaving anyone out?"

"No. I mean, no, you're wrong. Of course, everyone doesn't know. Hardly. . . anyone knows."

"And just how did Julie find out?" Kate demanded.

Rachel shrugged. "The only reason Julie knows is that I mentioned it in passing when we had lunch together today. We wanted you to join us, as well, but Kelly said you'd gone to lunch with Brody, so—"

"The point is that I wasn't informed," Kate said, cutting her sister off, wanting to forget about that lunch with Brody and all that had gone on before lunch back in Brody's office. "The point is that my opinion—never mind my approval—wasn't sought. I suppose Brody Baker's decided that what I think isn't of any consequence," Kate said sarcastically.

"Kate, you've got Brody all wrong. He knows he can't go ahead on any project without getting your okay. If you ask me, I think he's simply working overtime to impress you. He wants to floor you with a bunch of brilliant ideas, making sure, first, that he's got something solid enough. . . ."

Kate wasn't listening. She remained on her own fierce track. "After all, I'm only the head of this station. Why should I be informed? Why should anyone bother to tell me anything about what's being planned? Get my input, not to mention my go-ahead?"

"Now, Kate, I just explained that. You're getting all worked up—"

"I am *not* worked up. Any more than I am turned on. And I am not going to sit quietly back and let those broken-down boots of Brody Baker's just walk right over me!"

Which was how Kate wound up going to Rachel's house for dinner that evening.

"IS THE LAMB TOO RARE?" Rachel asked her sister solicitously. "Because if it is, I could cut you off some slices from the other end."

Brody, who was sitting across the oval teak table from Kate in the Parker dining room, plucked two slices of the thin-sliced meat from his plate.

"Here," he said, reaching across and depositing them on Kate's plate. "These are a little less pink."

"Did I say I wanted them less pink? No. No, I didn't. But why even bother to find out what I have to say?"

"I was just . . ." Brody started to protest mildly.

Kate cut him off. "You just go your merry way and take matters into your own hands. You just take it upon yourself to . . ."

"Now, hold on, Kate."

"No. You hold on, Brody. And I mean *hold on*."

"Look, if you're going to start mixing apples and oranges again—"

"Oh no, you're not going to pull that one again."

"Hey, all I did was offer you—"

"Offer me? Did you say 'offer me'? Let me tell you something, Brody—"

Rachel sprang up from her chair. "I think I forgot the...the brussels sprouts. In the kitchen." She looked pointedly over at her husband. "Um... darling, could you help me with the brussels sprouts?"

Delaney grinned as he rose from the table. "Right. Sure. The brussels sprouts. They can be a handful, all right."

Kate was up on her feet before Delaney finished. "No. I'll help Rachel with the brussels sprouts."

"Oh no," Rachel said quickly, sitting back down. "I mean..." She compressed her lips and frowned. "What was I thinking? I didn't make the brussels sprouts tonight. I made them last night. Isn't that right, Delaney? Wasn't it yesterday we made the brussels sprouts?"

Delaney's grin remained intact. "Now that you mention it, Rach, I do believe we did have brussels sprouts yesterday. Brussels sprouts and chicken, right?"

"Right," Rachel said. "Brussels sprouts and chicken. And those nice little red potatoes."

"How could I forget those potatoes," Delaney said, giving his stomach a little pat.

Absolute silence followed. Kate stared down at her plate. Brody stared across at Kate. Delaney blithely cut off a piece of lamb and popped it into his mouth. Rachel sat there trying to think up some other excuse to provide Kate and Brody with a chance to have a private tête-à-tête. A new idea came to her.

"Was that Samantha?" Rachel asked with mock concern. "Did anyone else just hear her cry?"

"No," Kate said succinctly.

"I'd better check," Rachel said, eyeing her husband again.

Before the words were out of his wife's mouth, Delaney, who could never be accused of being slow on the uptake, was on his feet again. "I'd better check with you," he said. "That Sam. She can be a handful, all right."

Kate rolled her eyes as the pair took off. "Really," she grumbled. "I don't think they could be more obvious if they hung out a sign."

"What's got you in such a tizzy, Kate?" Brody asked softly.

Kate debated saying anything, but that was why she'd shown up for dinner. To give Brody Baker a piece of her mind. What little of it she had left.

"I resent what you're doing," she responded in a tightly controlled voice.

Brody arched a brow. "Eating?"

"Taking over."

"Taking over what?"

"Everything."

"Could you be a little more specific?"

"You never once mentioned this crime segment with Delaney to me, for starters."

Brody ran his thumb across his lips. "Are you sure that's where you want to start?"

Kate glared at him. "What is that supposed to be? Some symbolic gesture?"

Brody looked baffled.

Kate imitated his hand movement, running her finger across her lips.

Brody gave her an innocent look. "I swear, Kate, nothing symbolic intended. It was just . . . I didn't even know I was doing it."

"All right," she said, ignoring his denial. "Let's start with that kiss."

Brody's blue eyes sparkled. "Which one?"

Kate glowered even though she knew it wasn't an altogether unreasonable question. Okay, so she'd suffered a momentary lapse of sanity. The point was she was perfectly sane now. And she was determined to hold on to her sanity. If only he didn't look so damn sexy. If only she could erase those sensations that had stirred within her when they'd kissed so passionately. She didn't want to stir things up. She didn't want to feel those feelings. They were dangerous. They'd only led to heartache in the past. After that fiasco with Oscar, she'd vowed to stay clear of intimate relationships with men. Some women were just better off without them. And she was one of them.

"I want to make one thing perfectly clear," she said evenly. Having firmed up her resolve, she looked Brody straight in the eye only to find herself thinking that eyes that blue ought to be outlawed. She dropped her gaze so as not to be distracted from her purpose, only for it to focus on his lips. Unfortunately, Brody's lips were no less devastating than his eyes. Things were going from bad to worse. Or good to better, depending on your perspective. At the moment, Kate's perspective was becoming increasingly skewed. Somehow, she couldn't look away from his mouth. Any more than she could keep herself from remembering how his mouth had felt on hers or how much she had wanted that kiss.

Had that been all she'd wanted? What if Mr. Fix-It hadn't shown up at that fateful moment? Where would that kiss have led?

"You were saying?"

Brody's voice brought Kate up short. She was saying something. What the hell was it?

Amusement danced in his eyes. "You were doing a Nixon imitation."

Kate screwed up her face. "A . . . what?"

"President Nixon. 'I want to make one thing perfectly clear.'" He did a fair imitation himself.

She gave her head a little shake, hoping to clear it. "What I wanted to say is simply this." She avoided his face altogether, fixing her gaze somewhere along his right shoulder. "I do not want to have a . . . a romantic involvement with you, Brody. If I . . . misled you in any way, I'm sorry."

She very carefully edged her plate a few inches away from her, folded her hands on the edge of the table, sat very straight in her chair and sighed heavily. "It should never have happened, but there's no point in haranguing myself about it. It did. It was no big deal. What I mean is, under other circumstances . . ."

"Other circumstances?"

"If we weren't . . . If I wasn't . . . If you weren't . . ."

She shut her eyes in frustration. Was she so far gone that she couldn't even make a simple declarative statement? Was she or wasn't she the woman who had vowed that she was through with men? One kiss and she'd turned into a blathering idiot. Think what a man like Brody Baker could do to her mental state if she gave him half a chance.

This time, when she looked him straight in the eye, she didn't flinch. "As far as we're concerned," she said firmly, "there are no other possible circumstances. And if you think there ever might be, you're going to be sorely disappointed. Because what happened this morning is never going to happen again."

She waited expectantly for a smart-aleck remark from Brody. A dare, even. When he made no response at all, she felt almost giddily grateful. Maybe Brody was capable of being more adult than she'd given him credit for. She even managed a little smile.

"There, now that that's . . . out of the way, I want to establish certain work . . . protocols," she said, pressing her palms together, pleased that her voice sounded reassuringly neutral and professional. Even if her heartbeat was racing a bit.

"And by that," she went on quickly, afraid she'd lose her train of thought, as seemed to happen so often around her program director, "I mean that I want you to cue me in on any program ideas that 'hit you in the face' before you go off, helter-skelter. . . ."

A mischievous smile tilted one corner of his mouth. "You are a great kisser, Katie."

Her hands flew apart, rose off the table like they were clutching a ball of air and then fell limply to her sides. So much for fooling herself into believing the man had the slightest capability of being adult about this.

"Why are you doing this to me, Brody?" she asked plaintively.

His hand went up to his heart. "What about what you're doing to me, Katie? Whatever else you say, you can't tell me, after the way you kissed me this morning, that you still give no credence to chemistry."

Just as Brody leaned forward and reached for Kate's hands, Rachel and Delaney appeared at the archway to the dining room. It was clear to both of them that their timing couldn't have been worse.

"The whipped cream. We've got to whip up that cream. For the dessert," Rachel said hurriedly, grabbing Delaney's shirtsleeve. "That is, I'll whip the cream while you . . . get the coffee up, darling."

"Will you both please sit down and just eat your dinner," Kate said sharply, only to pop up herself.

"Where are you going?" Rachel asked in confusion.

"Home," Kate said and strode across the room.

Brody jumped up a few seconds later and took off after Kate.

The door slammed once. Then a second time. Rachel looked at Delaney. Delaney looked at Rachel.

"I'd call it progress," Rachel mused.

"I'd call it war," Delaney countered with a smile.

"Exactly," Rachel said with a grin.

SKYE WAS AT THE kitchen table doing her homework when her mom stormed into the room through the back door. She was mumbling under her breath. Skye reflected that she did that a lot lately. Namely, ever since Brody Baker had hit town.

"Hi," Skye said, watching her mom head straight across the room for the swing door.

"I'm going upstairs," Kate muttered. "I need to lie down. I need . . . some peace and quiet. I'm all wound up."

"You should try yoga, Mom."

"Karate's more what I need," Kate said dryly.

"No, seriously, Mom. You could participate with Mrs. Cromwell, Julie and Ben. Even Rachel's going to check with her obstetrician and see if she can do it. And Brody says I can come to the Saturday-morning class. . . ."

Kate stopped in her tracks and swung around to her daughter. "Did you say Brody?"

It was as if Skye had said a dirty word.

"It isn't really set yet," Skye said hesitantly. "Actually, he's waiting for an answer from Louisa Carpenter."

"Louisa Carpenter?" Kate uttered the name between clenched teeth.

"She's really into yoga, Mom. Remember she ran that yoga class at the rec center last year. Brody thought she could do a morning yoga show and that anyone on the staff could participate. Kind of to demonstrate that anyone can do it." Skye giggled. "Somehow, I can't picture Meg Cromwell in a lotus position. Can you, Mom?"

Kate threw her hands up in the air. "I don't believe this. I just don't believe this." Without another word she flung open the kitchen's swing door and strode out. No sooner had the door swung back than the front doorbell rang. On her way to see who was there, Skye collided with her mom in the front hall.

"Don't answer it," Kate ordered.

"Don't answer it?" Skye echoed, giving her mother a baffled look.

The doorbell rang again.

"Oh, that man is impossible," Kate said, regarding the closed door with fierce determination. "He simply refuses to quit."

The bell rang a third time, then was followed by a plaintive shout. "Kate. Kate, would you please let me in?"

Skye looked at her mom. "That sounds like Brody Baker."

"That's because it *is* Brody Baker," Kate muttered, heading for the stairs. "I'm going up to my room."

"Kate. I know you're in there. I'm not going away until . . ."

Skye heard her mother's bedroom door slam as she opened the front door and gave Brody a sympathetic smile. "I don't think she wants to see you right now, Mr. Baker."

"I told you last time I saw you down at the station that you can call me Brody, Skye."

"Brody. That's a neat name."

"So's Skye. Bet your mom picked it out."

"Dad wanted to call me Margaret. Can you imagine? Margaret?" She made a face.

Brody laughed. "Good thing your mom got her way."

"She's pretty good at that. Most of the time."

Brody sighed as he leaned against the doorjamb. "You have her figured out?"

Skye laughed. "Usually. But sometimes she surprises you."

"Out of the mouths of babes," Brody murmured, his face breaking into a smile.

"Hey, I'm fourteen and a quarter."

Brody grinned. "Sorry. It was just an expression. You are indeed very grown-up."

Skye frowned. "I wish my mom would realize that." She was still upset that her mother had never told her about her parents' unique alimony arrangement.

"Moms can be like that. Sometimes my mother treats me like a kid."

"Where is your mom?" Skye asked.

"In Texas. Just outside of San Antonio."

"Is that where you were brought up? Texas?"

"Texas, Arkansas, New Mexico, Arizona. My dad was an oilman. We traveled a lot. Never did really get to settle down. I envy you being all your life in one place. And a nice little place it is."

"Pittsville? You really think so?"

Brody smiled wistfully. "Yep. I really think so."

Skye observed him thoughtfully. "It isn't just Pittsville that you like, though, is it?"

"Did you say you were only fourteen?" Brody teased. But then his expression turned serious. "No. It isn't just Pittsville. It's . . . your mom, too."

Skye nodded. "Everyone's pretty much figured that out."

Brody eyed her. "And how does 'everyone' feel about it?"

"You mean Mom?"

"Well, actually, I was thinking about you."

Skye's face clouded.

"It bothers you?" Brody asked anxiously.

Brody's question immediately brought the alimony situation to Skye's mind. Should she say something about it to Brody? Should she tell him that if he had any hopes of one day marrying her mom, chances were pretty slim because it would mean her losing WPIT? The more Skye thought about it, the more she believed her mother wouldn't let the station go. Partly because she really loved it, partly because it "brought home the bacon," as her Grandpa Leo always said; and not just for the two of them, but her two sisters had a big stake in it, as well. It was more than that, though. No matter how much her mom might care about Brody, even be wild about him, would she ever trust him? After her dad? After that creep, Oscar Foote? It didn't seem fair to Skye that Brody should be punished for the way someone else had treated her mom. But then how often had she heard her mom say, "Who ever said life was fair?"

Brody was watching Kate's daughter closely. "Skye, I just want you to know that I'd never do anything to intentionally hurt your mom. Or you."

Skye gave him a level look. "I can take care of myself. But my mom . . . Well, she makes you think she's real tough and all, only don't let that fool you."

"I don't," he said solemnly. "I really do think your mom's terrific."

Skye nodded. "I think so, too. Even if we don't always see eye-to-eye on everything . . ."

Brody grinned. "Tell me about it."

Skye hesitated. "Which reminds me, I think she's a little miffed that you didn't tell her about the yoga show."

"I seem to have getting her miffed down to a science. I guess I shouldn't have gone and put all my carts before the horse."

Skye glanced up the stairs in the direction of her mother's bedroom. "I guess not."

Brody followed Skye's gaze. "I don't suppose there's any point in trying to get her to come down and hash things out tonight. . . ."

"In my experience," Skye said sagely, "it's better to let her cool off first."

He nodded and started to turn away from the door, but then glanced back at Skye. "Say, you wouldn't happen to know what your mom's favorite flowers—"

"Tulips. She's wild about tulips."

Brody smiled. "Tulips. Hmm. Oh, one other question . . ."

November 6

It's love. I know it. Brody's in love with my mom. And he's so neat. We ended up talking for close to an hour tonight. Not just about what kind of flowers and other stuff that Mom likes, but he told me stuff about himself and asked me stuff about myself. And it wasn't like with some grown-ups when they ask you questions and they really don't care about your answers. Brody really wanted to know—things like why my history teacher drove me nuts, what qualities in a friend did I think were important, what I wanted to study in college. I told him that I wanted to be a journalist and he told me that his sister, Annie, wrote for the San Francisco *Gazette*. Well, she wrote a nutrition column for them. Brody said it was Annie who got him interested in cooking. She's three years older than him, and married, with two kids.

That's another thing—Brody's crazy about kids. He says he'd like to have at least two when he gets married. And he gave me this certain look, like he definitely had it in mind exactly who he wanted to marry and have those kids with.

I remember one time when I was about seven—not long before Mom and Dad split up—I overheard this fight between them where Mom was saying stuff about having wanted to have more children and being angry at my dad because he didn't. Pretty ironic, considering that once Dad remarried, he ended up having three kids with Sue Ellen.

As Mom would say, Men! Only I don't think Brody's like the "men" Mom means when she says, "Men." Not only that. I don't think Mom thinks so, either, which is part of what's got her in such a tizzy. The other part is Brody himself.

The thing is, if Brody and Mom ever do tie the knot, there's no reason why she couldn't have more kids. She's still plenty young enough to do it. And it would be real neat having a baby sister or brother. Or both. I love being an aunt, but being a big sister's even better. It would be a real special bond.

Whoa, as Grandpa Leo would say. I'm putting the cart before the horse. The horse being WPIT. And I guess the cart being my dad and my Grandma Agnes. I just feel it in my bones (another of Grandpa Leo's phrases) that Mom won't allow herself to admit her feelings for Brody, much less ever consider marrying him, if it means giving up the station.

I'm thinking, maybe I should drop by Grandma Agnes's house and see if we couldn't have a little heart-to-heart. Okay, so we never have before, but I'm a lot older now. And Mom says I can be real persuasive when I put my mind to something. Maybe I can get my grandmother to talk to my dad about this dumb alimony arrangement. He wouldn't listen to me (in his eyes I'm still a kid), but he might listen to his mother. I usually listen to mine—even if I do sometimes give her a little grief before I do. Maybe there's some way to get my grandma and my dad to see that it just wouldn't be fair for Mom and Aunt Julie and Aunt Rachel and Ben and Brody to have to lose everything they've worked so hard for just because Mom and Brody are in love and want to get married. I know, deep down, my dad doesn't care a hoot about the station. He never really did.

Unfortunately, my grandma does care. So she's really the one I'll have to convince if I'm ever going to get her to convince my dad to let Mom keep WPIT and live happily ever after with Brody.

WHEN KATE ARRIVED in her office the next morning she was flabbergasted to discover a veritable sea of multicolored tulips covering practically every inch of the room. She felt as if she'd stepped into a garden smack dab in the middle of Holland.

"What the . . . ?"

Meg Cromwell came up behind Kate. "Aren't they fantastic?"

Kate looked over her shoulder at the television chef. "What do you know about these?"

Meg smiled impishly. "Why don't you read the card? Or should I say cards?"

As Kate scrutinized the dozens of bouquets of flowers set in vases of every shape and size dispersed all around her office, she saw that there was a note attached to each bouquet.

"Wow," Julie said, coming up behind Meg. She called down the hall to Ben. "Hey, babe. Come here. You've got to see these."

Ben, who was having a chat with Gus, headed over with the stage manager toward Kate's office. Rachel, who was just coming in the door, followed the pair.

Kate turned to the group that had gathered, jockeying for space outside her door. "Okay, this isn't a garden party. Don't you all have . . . work to do?"

Julie nudged Ben, who nudged Rachel, who nudged Gus, who nudged Meg. The group reluctantly started to saunter off when Kate called them to a halt. They all stopped on a dime.

Kate strode around her office, snatching off the notes pinned to each of the bouquets of tulips. Without a second look, she deposited the collection into her trash. Then she turned to the group who'd all clustered again at her open office door.

"Each of you—grab as many vases as you can. I want all these flowers cleared out of here."

"What should we do with them?" Meg asked.

Kate scowled. "I don't know. I really don't care. I just want them out of my sight. You can throw the whole lot of them in the Dumpster out back as far as I'm concerned."

"These must have cost a fortune," Meg protested. "It would be absolutely criminal to throw them out."

"All right, all right," Kate conceded. "Put them...put them in the studio as a backdrop. Maybe you can make something with a Dutch theme for your cooking show this week. I don't care what you do with them. Just get them out of here."

As soon as the group left, their arms loaded with vases of tulips, Kate stepped into her office and shut the door firmly behind her. She knew, without opening a single card, that this had to be Brody's doing. Well, if he thought she'd be placated by a bunch of flowers—okay, by a lot of bunches of flowers . . .

She stared down at the wastebasket. No, she told herself. It doesn't matter what he wrote on those notes. She started across the room for her desk, stopped and turned back to the wastebasket.

"Damn," she muttered under her breath.

She plucked one note out of the trash, debated for a couple of seconds even though she knew she'd already lost the battle. She started to read the note, expecting a few simple words of apology. As if anything Brody Baker ever did was simple. Or predictable.

Instead of a plain, ordinary "I'm sorry" scribbled on the paper, Kate found a snippet of one of her favorite Robert Browning poems.

One by one, Kate collected all the notes out of the wastebasket and read them in turn. More Browning snippets.

She sat down at her desk. On top of a stack of files, memos and reports was another envelope with her name written across it in what she recognized as Brody's handwriting. She opened it and took out several sheets of paper that outlined in detail the plans her new program director had both for new shows and for restructuring formats and scheduling for existing shows.

She was nearly finished reading when she was interrupted by a knock on her door.

"Come in," she called out distractedly.

"Hi."

Kate looked up from Brody's notes to see Louisa Carpenter standing at her open door. The svelte redhead looked like she'd had to be shoehorned into her electric-blue and sunshine-yellow Lycra biking pants and matching, hip-hugging jacket. Even her bicycle helmet, which was tucked under one arm, was color coordinated.

"I was looking for Brody," Louisa said in her inimitably husky Marilyn Monroe voice that perfectly matched her Marilyn Monroe body.

Whatever Kate might think of Louisa Carpenter, there was no denying that the three-time divorcée was "stacked"—as her ex-husband, Arnie, had remarked with enough frequency during their marriage to make Kate think he might have "dabbled" with the redheaded sexpot before he'd gotten involved with his receptionist.

"Mr. Baker's got his own office," Kate said tartly.

Louisa trilled a laugh. "That's very funny, Kate. His own office. I didn't honestly think you two were *bunking* together," she added with a little titter.

Kate did not share Louisa's amusement.

"It's down the hall. Last door on the right."

Louisa fluffed up her long, lush red hair with her fingers, then posed one hand on her jutting hip. "Or am I wrong? I have been hearing some rumors floating around about you and Brody."

Kate could feel all her muscles stiffen.

Louisa trilled another little laugh. It sent the same kind of shivers up Kate's spine as did the sound of fingernails scratching on a blackboard.

"Usually I say where there's smoke there's fire, if you know what I mean," Louisa drawled.

Kate's mouth tightened, but she didn't say a word.

Louisa's ruby-red lips shifted from a cunning smile to a smirk. "But in this case, it's just too hard to believe. I mean, it's like mixing lemons with heavy cream."

Kate had a good idea who the lemon was supposed to be.

"Or like—"

Kate cut her off at the quick. "I think I get the point, Louisa."

"So there isn't anything to the rumors?"

"I don't pay attention to rumors. I have all I can handle running this station and raising my daughter. Everything else is . . . superfluous."

Louisa clearly appeared pleased with Kate's response. "I suppose Brody told you about my doing the yoga show."

"He submitted the proposal to me for my consideration," Kate corrected, eyeing the sheet of paper in front of her.

"He's been after me for days. Brody Baker is a man who simply doesn't take no for an answer."

Tell me about it, Kate thought.

"The man finally wore me down," Louisa simpered. "I just couldn't resist. So last night I finally agreed to do it."

"Last night?" The words escaped Kate's lips before she could stop them.

"Yes. He dropped by my place around nine. No, actually it was closer to ten. And heaven only knows what time it was when he finally left." Louisa yawned delicately, then moistened her lips with the tip of her tongue.

Kate was reminded of a cat in heat.

Louisa gave her hair another pouf. "Only I absolutely insisted that he'd have to give me a few weeks so I could lose these five absolutely unsightly pounds before I go prancing around in my leotard in front of the cameras," she proclaimed, patting her nonexistent tummy.

Kate gave the obnoxious woman a cool study. "Only five?"

6

AT FIRST KATE THOUGHT she was imagining it. Faint sounds. Almost . . . moans. She gave her head a shake and continued making program notes.

The sounds grew louder. Frowning, Kate set her pen down on her desk. What the hell was it?

She got up, went over to her door, opened it and looked out into the anteroom to see if Kelly had any idea. Kelly was standing at the open door leading out into the hall.

"What is it?" Kate asked.

At the sound of Kate's voice, Kelly spun around and, looking exceedingly flustered, slammed the door.

"Uh . . . nothing," Kelly mumbled.

Kate raised an eyebrow as she strode across the room and reopened the door only to discover Meg, Gus, Julie, Ben and Rachel in the hall looking like a mini-football team huddled together as if to decide on their next play.

As Kate eyed the group suspiciously, a distinct, drawn-out moan filtered down the hall. There was no question where the moan was coming from. All eyes, including Kate's, shifted in the direction of Brody's office.

"O-o-oh. No. No, wait, darling," a husky voice cried out. There was no question whose voice it was. Louisa Carpenter's.

"Please, just let me try..." Brody countered, loud and clear.

The group in the hall now noticed Kate. They stared at her in silence, all of them looking exceedingly uncomfortable. Kate stared back at them, equally speechless.

The only ones talking were Brody and Louisa.

"If you just move your foot up a little, Brody..."

"If I lift it any higher I'm going to—" Brody cut off his sentence with another moan.

Kate stood there riveted to the spot, awash in a mixture of mortification, fury and despair. How could he? One minute he was showering her with flowers and poetry and the next minute he was down there in his office playing footsie—to put it discreetly—with another woman. Oh, sure, it was obvious to Kate that Louisa intended to make a grandstand play for Brody, but that he would succumb to that sexpot's wiles so quickly, so easily, so blatantly, right there at the station...

"Darling, don't arch your back."

"Louisa, just move your hand a little lower...."

Julie broke from the group, averting her gaze from her sister. "This is too much," she declared, her voice dripping with righteous indignation. "I am going to put a stop to this . . . this whatever, this very instant."

Kate started to argue, but Julie was determined and the rest of the group all supported Julie's decision. They marched right down the hall after Julie, who, without even knocking, heedlessly threw open Brody's door. "Now look here—"

Julie stopped abruptly, stared wide-eyed into the office and then, astonishing Kate, broke into gales of laughter. No sooner had Julie stepped aside so that the others had the opportunity to peer inside, than they, too, began to crack up.

Kate couldn't believe what she was witnessing. Why in heaven's name were they all laughing? Curiosity propelled her down the hall to Brody's office. Still laughing, everyone cleared away from the open door as she approached.

Kate peered inside. She didn't laugh. She was simply too flabbergasted. There was Brody sitting on his Navajo rug in the middle of his office, looking for all the world like a *pretzel*. And not looking very happy about it. And there was Louisa kneeling before him, looking very dismayed. She glanced back at Kate.

"He was trying the lotus position. Only it seems he got a little . . . stuck."

"I am not stuck," Brody snapped. "Something pulled in my back."

"You're tensing up," Louisa scolded him. "You must try to wrap yourself in calm, darling. Try to visualize yourself as an empty container with air slowly pouring in—"

"Louisa," Brody growled.

She shrugged. "I'm only trying to help. Yoga is a mind-body experience and—"

"Stop, stop," Brody pleaded.

Kate bit back a grin. "Louisa, I don't think this is helping Brody relax."

Grimacing and wincing, Brody freed his left foot, which was wedged high on his right thigh. He swatted Louisa's hand away as she tried to assist him with his right foot. Once he'd untangled his legs he bent forward in pain, both palms pressing into his lower back.

"Brody, just listen to how you're breathing," Louisa continued her spiel. "It's so agitated and unrhythmic.

Now, if you'd just let me guide you into a positive, constructive image, I can help you get your breathing under control. It's all a matter of enjoining your epigastric plexus and your solar plexus. . . ."

While Louisa prattled on, Brody looked over at Kate, his expression imploring.

Julie, who was standing behind Kate, gave her sister a little shove, setting her in motion. Kate stepped into the office and went over to Louisa, who was still kneeling on the floor, and took hold of her arm. "I really think Brody needs a little time to himself."

"You're right. Absolutely," Brody quickly agreed with Kate.

"But, darling," Louisa persisted, a screechy whine sneaking into her usually throaty voice, "I can fix your back up in a jiffy if you'll just—"

"No, really," Brody protested. "This has happened to me before and all I need is what Kate said—a little time to myself."

Kate tugged the resistant woman to her feet. "I'm sure he'll be okay, Louisa."

Forcing a smile, Brody nodded. "Yep. It's . . . it's feeling better already."

"Smiling's good," Louisa said, beaming back at Brody, even as Kate was ushering her to the door. "Smiling and controlled breathing are essential elements—"

Kate shut the door on the yoga teacher as she continued with, "For taking into our bodies cosmic perfection and inspiration."

Kate and Brody could still hear Louisa chattering away about the benefits of yoga as she was being hustled down the hall and finally out the front door by the WPIT staff.

Once they were alone, Brody closed his eyes, sighed and shook his head. "Do me a favor."

Kate looked down at him. "Help you up?"

"Help me up? Are you kidding? I may never get up again. I may never move again. No. The favor is, cross that nutty yoga-class idea off my list."

Kate knelt down to Brody's level, the corners of her mouth curling in a smile. "Are you sure?"

"You find this funny, huh?" he muttered.

Kate's smile deepened. "No. No, of course it isn't funny."

"I happen to be in pain here," he said between clenched teeth as he slowly, painfully, curled over and stretched out on his stomach across his Navajo rug.

Kate felt guilty for being amused at Brody's expense and erased the smile. "I'm sorry. Really, is there anything I can do to help?"

"I suppose you could try massaging my back."

"Are you sure you wouldn't rather have me call a chiropractor. Lyle Goldsmith has an office right here in town and I'm sure—"

"What's the matter, Kate? Afraid you'll lose control again?" Brody quipped.

"Oh, come off it, Brody."

"Hey, all I'm saying is if you think you can't keep yourself from—"

"You may be having a problem with your back, but there's certainly nothing wrong with your ego."

"Right there at the base of my spine."

Kate hesitated. "I'm not very good at this."

"My problem may be having too much self-confidence, yours is having too little."

"I happen to be an extremely confident woman," she argued. "Just not when it comes to . . ."

"Men?" Brody smirked.

"Massages."

The smirk on his face melted into a smile. "You might find you're better at it than you ever guessed."

"You're too much, Brody," she said, giving in. "Now, where does it hurt?"

"Just start at the bottom and work your way up. Or start at the top and work your way down."

Kate dropped to her knees beside him, then compressed her lips as she stared down at his back. Damn, she was a little nervous about touching him, massaging his muscles, getting on such *intimate* terms with his body. What if she lost control? Again?

No, she told herself. That was nuts. She had to get a grip on herself. After all, she was a rational, sensible woman and she'd made a firm decision about not wanting to get romantically involved with any man. Especially a man like Brody Baker. If he thought he could simply barge into her life and turn it topsy-turvy...

Okay, so she had felt a little spark of jealousy when she'd thought that he and Louisa Carpenter were fooling around in here. She quickly told herself it wasn't really so much jealousy as indignation. Righteous indignation. It was so inappropriate, so indiscreet, in such poor taste. And, she admitted, it had seemed like a slap in the face, after having just filled her office with all those tulips and poetry.

Only they hadn't been fooling around. So she'd been wrong about Brody. Damn the man. It would have been so much easier if she'd been right about him. Why couldn't he have been like other men? Then she could have been outraged and written him off. It would have made her life so much easier.

"I think you need to press a little harder," he teased, considering that she still had yet to put so much as a finger on him.

Gritting her teeth, she placed her hands on his back and, with a hard, circular motion, began digging her fingers into his muscles.

He let out a little cry.

"See, I told you I should call in a chiropractor," she charged.

"No, no. You're doing great."

"Your muscles are really knotted up," she admitted, after administering to him for a few moments.

"Did you think I was lying? A ploy to seduce you?"

"What about those flowers? Was that a ploy?" she asked, finding herself caught up in her ministrations. Too caught up?

"That was an apology."

"Do you always . . . apologize so . . . grandiosely?"

"No. No, I don't," he said simply.

Kate scowled as she stared down at his back. "I'm sure there must have been times, though.... Women..."

"You don't have to beat around the bush, you know. If you want to know about the women in my life—"

"I don't," she said adamantly, digging her fingers harder into his muscles. This time when he cried out, she knew she had hurt him. He really did madden her.

"Could you go a little lower?"

She was already at the base of his spine. "I don't think so."

He turned his head to the side and gave her a slow smile. "It's written all over your face, Katie."

"What's written all over my face?" Absently her hands had inched lower, her fingers, seemingly of their own accord, dipping slightly past the waistband of his gray cords.

Instead of answering her, he whispered, "You have a great face."

She felt ridiculously flattered. No one had ever given her face much credit. Her breath quickened, and her own muscles, in contrast to Brody's, were beginning to feel loose and fluid.

Brody emitted a soft moan. It was only after the sound registered that Kate realized the cause of it. Her hands had found their way under his shirt; her fingers were now pressing into his bare flesh.

What was she doing? Instantly her hands sprang off him.

Slowly, Brody rolled over onto his back. The expression in his renegade blue eyes was so piercing, Kate felt immobilized. Now, instead of her breathing quickening, it stopped altogether. Everything seemed to stop.

Everything, that is, except Brody's hands. He lifted them up to her face. Kate closed her eyes.

"I think I'm falling in love with you, Kate Hart," he murmured.

"I've got...to go," she protested, not moving an inch, not opening her eyes. "I've got . . . a lot on my mind."

"Am I on your mind?"

"No." But she was nodding her head.

One of his hands seemed to move in slow motion from her flushed cheek down over her throat and then still lower. She needed to tell him to stop, but her throat was dry and even though her lips parted, not a sound escaped.

Until his hand moved lightly over her breast.

"O-o-oh."

"Am I here, Kate? Here in your heart?" He lifted himself up onto one elbow and placed his warm mouth on the soft fabric of her blouse over her nipple. Even through the silk blouse and her lacy bra she could feel his heated breath, feel her nipple snap to attention like a duplicitous soldier gone over to the enemy camp. Traitor.

"Your . . . back. Really, Brody . . . you should . . . be careful," she stammered.

"I don't want to be careful. I don't want to play it safe. I don't want to put life on hold, Kate. Carpe diem. Seize the day."

A spiral of desire curled through Kate's body, but her mind was still struggling to fend it off. "That's all right for you," she said in a weak voice, having to gather all her willpower to move away from him. She clutched her hands in her lap to keep from reaching out and pulling him back to her breast.

He looked up at her, smiling, his long rebel's hair falling around his face.

"What's so funny?" she demanded.

"I was just thinking about the look on your face when you saw me and Louisa in here."

"Well . . . it's not every day you find your program director stuck in a . . . in a yoga position on the floor."

Brody let his gaze drift appreciatively over her. "Louisa Carpenter isn't my type, Kate."

Kate tried to pretend not to notice. Just as she tried to pretend to be unaffected. She knew she wasn't being too successful at either. "I never thought . . . I never said she was."

He leaned closer to her. Their mouths were only inches apart. "*You're* my type, Kate." His tongue darted out and stroked her lips.

"No," she whimpered. "We can't do this here."

He pressed his lips to her ear. "Then where?" he whispered.

"That's not...what I mean." Why had she said *here?* All she'd meant to say was, *We can't do this,* period.

"My place. Tonight."

"No. I can't. Skye... She's got... basketball practice." Why was she making excuses? Why didn't she simply tell him to stop trying to seduce her?

His mouth had slipped from her ear to her neck, where he proceeded to plant a row of tiny kisses. "Drop her off and then come over."

"I've got to go... grocery shopping then. There's... nothing in...my house. You should...see my... refrigerator."

"I don't want to see your refrigerator, Katie."

"It's pathetic. A frozen turkey potpie..."

"I want to see your body...."

She swallowed hard. "And neither Skye or I... even like turkey...."

"I want to slowly undress you by candlelight...."

"Moo Goo Gai Pan from the Chinese restaurant... that should have been... tossed out weeks ago..."

"I want to feast on the sight of you sprawled across my bed...."

Her breathing was ragged. "And...and several of Meg Cromwell's concoctions. Really...dreadful stuff..."

"Feel every delectable inch of your warm, soft flesh..."

Beads of perspiration dotted her forehead."This awful beef Stroganoff..."

"I want to press your body against mine...."

She had the oddest sensation that the floor was starting to tilt. "I really do . . . have to . . . so to the gore. Go to the store."

"I want to make wild, loud, messy love to you, Kate. . . ."

Her mouth opened, but no words came out.

"I want rockets to go off," he whispered. "I want us to soar up to Jupiter or Mars and then slip right over the edge of the whole damn galaxy."

A small pulse throbbed in her throat. Hell, her whole body was throbbing. Her insides were like marshmallows melting over a hot flame. And Brody was that flame.

"But, I guess," he murmured, "if you really have to 'so to the gore . . .'"

SKYE SHIFTED IN THE passenger seat of her mother's battered green Ford Escort and looked over at her mom as they drove over to the high-school gym for her basketball practice that evening. "You're awfully quiet tonight."

"Am I?"

"You didn't forget the list, did you?"

"The list?"

"The shopping list."

"Oh. That list."

"Well, did you?"

"Did I what?"

"Forget it."

Kate shrugged distractedly, her eyes glued to the road. "Fine."

Skye chuckled. "What did he do today?"

Kate almost slammed into the car in front of them, which was stopped for a red light. Her foot hit the brake hard.

"What did you hear?" Kate asked her daughter anxiously.

Aha, Skye thought. So something had happened. "I didn't hear anything, Mom." Not that she wasn't all ears. "Is there something you want to tell me?"

"No."

"You might feel better."

Kate rolled her eyes. "Aren't we reversing roles here?"

Skye grinned. "Aunt Rachel says that when a woman's in love she often acts like a schoolgirl."

"In love?" Kate echoed, flustered. "Well, she certainly couldn't have been talking about me."

"Oh, no," Skye said airily. "She was just talking in general."

"It's complete and utter nonsense."

The car in front of Kate's pulled out.

"The light, Mom."

"Love is not something a person...comes down with suddenly. Like a bad cold."

The car behind Kate's Escort gave a little honk.

"The light, Mom. It's green."

"Right. I see that," Kate muttered, stepping on the gas too abruptly and stalling.

The car behind her honked again.

"All right, all right," Kate snapped, restarting the engine.

"Oh, I almost forgot," Skye said, once they were moving again. "Alice and I have a project we're doing together for history. So, if it's okay with you, I was going to go over to her house after practice so we could work on it. Alice's mom will pick us up and she already told Alice she'd give me a lift home. I won't be later than ten o'clock. Is that okay, Mom?"

Kate cleared her throat. "Ten o'clock?"

"We'll be done with practice by eight-thirty and that'll give us over an hour to do this dumb map we've got to do."

Kate's mind was racing overtime. It wasn't quite seven. Skye wouldn't be home until ten. Three hours. Three *free* hours. Her heart was beating wildly, in sharp contrast to the steady drone of the engine.

"That'll give you plenty of time to shop. Not that you love going grocery shopping..."

"One doesn't have to love grocery shopping. Grocery shopping is a responsibility. It's an obligation."

"Mom."

"It's something that...has to get done. And... somebody has to do it."

"Mom."

"I have to do it. I have to do it because...because I'm a responsible person. I'm a parent...a single parent, at that. I have to see to it that everything's in order, that our lives are running smoothly..."

"Mom," Skye said sharply this time.

"What is it?"

"You just passed the high school."

KATE USUALLY SHOPPED in town at Cobb's Grocery Store, but tonight she deliberately drove the extra half hour over to the Grand Market at the plaza in Louden. Just as she'd deliberately changed after work into a pair of grubby jeans and an oversize and decidedly unflattering thick gray sweatshirt.

She grabbed one of the few remaining shopping carts parked outside the market and strode into the large, brightly fluorescent-lit building, pausing just inside the entrance.

Her shopping list. Where was her shopping list? She rummaged through her bag. Damn. She could see it now, right there on her refrigerator door where she'd left it.

Now what would Freud have said about that? Hell, she didn't need a psychiatrist to decipher the meaning. So what if she was feeling ambivalent. Brody Baker did hold a certain primitive appeal. As Skye had so succinctly put it, he was a "hunk." The kind of hunk that was plastered all over those romance sagas that she kept finding in her daughter's room, tucked in between books like *Animal Farm* and *To Kill a Mockingbird*.

Well, Brody might be a dashing, sexy, renegade hero, but she was no sultry, drop-dead-gorgeous heroine. She was a plain, no-nonsense thirty-five-year-old woman with a fourteen-year-old child to raise. And a television station to run.

Was that the rub? WPIT? This past summer when she'd allowed herself to get caught up in that ridiculous romance with Oscar, and he'd even had the audacity to broach marriage, she'd been reminded, really for the first time in ages, of her divorce agreement. If she were to marry Oscar—or any man—it would mean giving ownership of the station back to Arnie. That was their arrangement—one she'd felt confident would never be challenged. Because she never intended to get married again. She may have briefly lost her head over Oscar, but deep down she'd sensed almost from their first meeting that there was something not quite right about him. Oscar's wife had arrived on the scene on the very evening Kate had planned to turn down his marriage proposal, realizing that what she felt for Oscar Foote wasn't love at all but merely foolish infatuation.

After their very public breakup, everyone, especially her family, had felt so badly for her because they'd thought Oscar had broken her heart. That wasn't it. She hated herself for having been taken in. And she'd solemnly vowed that it would never happen again.

What was it her dad was always saying about never say never?

"Excuse me," someone said from behind her.

Kate jumped. "What?"

A tired-looking young woman, whose jacket sleeve was being tugged by her pesky toddler, smiled apologetically at Kate. "I'm sorry. I didn't mean to startle you. I was just wondering if you were through with your cart or just getting started with it. There are no others left."

Kate stared from the woman to the child and back to her cart. She frowned. "Well... actually—" She stopped. "Why don't you go ahead and take it. I just need a few things." *Like getting my head examined.*

"Thanks," the appreciative shopper said with relief, as she hoisted her son into the front seat of the cart. "Isn't shopping a drag?" she remarked as she wheeled the cart off.

Kate watched the woman head down the aisle. Then she looked around the market. Shopping certainly was a drag. And it never felt more so than it did at that moment.

Of course, she did have other options. *I want to slowly undress you by candlelight. I want to make wild, loud, messy love to you, Kate....*

She shook her head vehemently, forcing her mind to concentrate on the task at hand. An older man was lifting two grocery bags full of food from his cart. "Here, young lady. You're looking mighty desperate. Take this cart."

Did she look desperate? "Oh. Oh, thanks." Not making a move, she stared at the emptied cart. "Actually..." *Take the cart, Kate. Take the cart, do your grocery shopping and then go home. You're a sensible woman and it's the sensible thing to do.*

"Actually," she began again, "I... I forgot my shopping list." She waved one arm in the air, indicating with a slight turn the electric-eye door leading out to the parking lot. "I'm just going to dash on home and...and get it."

A minute later, Kate sat behind the wheel of her hatchback, the ignition key in her hand. What was wrong with her? It was as if Brody Baker had opened a Pandora's box inside her and all kinds of wild and alien emotions were spilling out all over the place.

She knew that she should simply drive home and forget about the shopping. Forget about Brody Baker back there in his little cottage, lit by candlelight, a fire no doubt roaring in the hearth, and perhaps a bottle of champagne on ice. Maybe he'd even gone and whipped something up.

Oh, he'd whipped something up, all right. He'd whipped her into a veritable frenzy. How could she have allowed Brody to get her into such a state? How could she let herself even think about the possibility of driving over to his place?

She stuck the key in the ignition. *You're going home. You're going home and you're going to be fine. You hear me, Kate. You're going to be just fine and dandy.*

7

KATE PULLED UP TO the stop sign at the corner of Elm and South Ward streets. Her nice two-story white-shingled house lay two blocks straight ahead on Elm. The cottage Brody Baker had rented from Louisa Carpenter was situated five blocks to the right, on South Ward.

She stared at the stop sign. Suddenly her hand darted out and flicked the turn signal, making the right arrow on her dash blink on and off, on and off.

What am I doing? she wondered, as she obeyed the signal as if it somehow had her under its spell. *This is nuts.*

But she kept on going. One block, two, three, four, five.

She drove right past Louisa Carpenter's red colonial with the black shutters. Right past the long, winding driveway that led from the main house to the small, matching red guest cottage, now the home of Brody Baker.

One more block and Kate reached a dead end. She pulled her car over to the curb. Her white-knuckled hands were actually trembling.

A minute later she stepped out of the car. The chill early-November wind blew her hair every which way and cut through her sweatshirt. She remembered an old plaid wool hunting jacket stowed in her trunk. The hell with it, she decided, as she started walking.

It really was cold out. The wind whipped her hair in her eyes and made her wince. She imagined her nose was getting all red and she could feel the goose bumps popping up like chicken pox on her skin, which had a tendency to get blotchy anyway when she was chilled.

Brody's husky voice echoed in her mind. *I want to feast on the sight of you sprawled across my bed....*

Oh, she'd look a sight, all right.

HE STOOD THERE AT HIS open door, framed by the soft glow of candlelight behind him, wearing tight-fitting jeans, a crooked, bad-boy grin and nothing else. Bare-chested, with not so much as a goose bump marring that tawny, masculine flesh. The unfairness of it almost made Kate spin around and bolt back down the driveway. But that grin of his held her fixed.

"It... isn't what... you think," she said. The words came out in spurts because her teeth were chattering. It was only partly due to feeling chilled. She also felt as if the air had been squeezed out of her body.

"I think you need to come inside and warm up."

"I don't want to 'warm up.'"

"Fine," he said stepping aside.

"I came over here to... talk things out," she said as she brushed past him, walking right into a small, cozy living room whose walls were painted the color of nubby wheat and accented by the darker natural-oak woodwork. The furnishings were spare and simple—a wine-colored sofa and matching love seat, a round oak pedestal coffee table, a wall of bookshelves that were well stocked.

More than a dozen candles lit the room. There was a fire roaring in the hearth. And two wine goblets sat side by side on the mantel. Everything was just as she'd imagined. And then there was Brody himself, damn him, surpassing her creative visions.

Kate pushed her hair away from her face, tucking it behind her ears. She compressed her lips. They felt chapped. She hadn't even bothered to put on any lipstick—or any makeup at all. And that dumb, oversize sweatshirt. She felt like she was swimming in it.

Well, this is it, Brody. This is the real me. This is the real face you thought was so great this morning. This is the body you couldn't wait to caress. I'm here to make you see what a big mistake you made.

Maybe if she told herself that was what she was doing here enough times, she would even believe it.

Brody shut the door behind her.

"Could you please . . . go put a shirt on," she muttered, keeping her back to him. Not that the image of his sexy torso wasn't already emblazoned in her mind. No doubt she'd be haunted by it for many a night.

"I was just changing when you knocked," he said. "I didn't want to keep you waiting."

"I can wait." *Could she?*

She could feel him standing right behind her. If she leaned back a little . . .

"Pour yourself a glass of wine."

"No, thanks," she said stiffly. "I'll be driving back home in a . . . few minutes. I don't approve of drinking and driving. As a . . . parent, I feel I have to set a good example. Not that Skye's driving yet. She's only fourteen, but in another couple of years . . . She's growing so fast." *And I'm growing older by the minute. Older and more ridiculous. Why am I babbling?*

Brody hadn't moved an inch. She could actually feel his warm breath on the back of her head.

"Well, at least go warm yourself by the fire. Oh, I forgot. You don't want to warm up," he said playfully.

She turned around to face him, her eyes clouded with confusion. "Don't make fun of me, Brody. I feel ridiculous enough as it is."

He stepped toward her. "Don't feel ridiculous, Kate. I'm so glad you're here." There was nothing playful in his voice now. His tone, his expression, were etched with sincerity. And those blue eyes were glistening with longing.

Kate was overcome by self-consciousness. Her hands went to her windswept hair. "I look awful. And I know it."

"You couldn't look awful if you worked at it."

"I did sort of work at it," she found herself admitting, smiling.

"See what I mean?" he murmured, then leaned over and planted a light, tender kiss on her chapped lips.

Her heart started to thump. She didn't realize how very much she'd wanted that kiss until after he'd given it.

Get a grip on yourself, for heaven's sake.

Something to steady her frazzled nerves—that's what she needed. "Maybe I will have that…wine. Just a half a glass. Even less." She raised a hand to demonstrate how much, but Brody caught her hand in his and brought it to his lips. Meanwhile, his free hand gently traced the curve of her shoulder. He seemed in no hurry to go and put on his shirt.

The chill had evaporated from her body, replaced by a heat that felt like it was burning right through her. This wasn't going as planned. *Oh, yes, it is,* a little voice inside her head whispered.

Her gaze fixed on his bare chest, then slowly slipped down to his bare feet. "So you don't always wear those old cowboy boots of yours."

He laughed softly, seductively. "No, not always," he replied, cupping her face in his hands, his thumbs stroking across her cheeks, his eyes boring into her.

Her whole body shook at his touch and she couldn't stop herself from imagining Brody slowly undressing her, his large hands moving all over her body, his mouth hot and moist on her goose-bumpy skin. She clamped her mouth shut to prevent a moan from giving her away, feeling both very young and much too old, all at the same time.

"Brody, I . . ."

"Shh."

"I . . . think this was a mistake. I think I'd better go."

"Please stay. I can't remember the last time I wanted anything as much as I want you not to leave."

"Damn you, Brody. Why do you have to go and say things like that?" *And worse still, sound like you truly mean them.* "It isn't fair," she added weakly.

He smiled so endearingly, her heart actually fluttered. Then he drew her to him, her hands getting caught between her sweatshirt and his bare chest, as he kissed her again. And again. Hot, rough, wonderful kisses. She freed her hands and wrapped them around his bare back, his warm, smooth flesh.

It's only lust, she told herself. She was only *in lust.* It wasn't really all that serious. Love, that was something else all together. Love was serious. Love was something she simply couldn't afford. Literally as well as figuratively.

Meanwhile Brody was lifting her sweatshirt up over her head. She let out a little gasp.

"It's okay, Katie."

"No, it isn't. I'm not even wearing a pretty bra," she blurted out and then felt utterly idiotic.

He gave her a slow, easy smile. "Then we'll take it right off."

Kate sighed. "You always have a solution for everything."

He slipped his hands around to her back. There was no fumbling as he unfastened the catch of her bra. "I try. I try especially hard with you. You can't even begin to imagine the kinds of exciting ideas you spark in me, Katie."

She clutched her unfastened bra against her breasts. "Why me, Brody? Why me?" She really couldn't fathom his attraction to her.

Incredulously, as she looked up into his bluer-than-blue eyes, she saw that they were actually misty.

"You're asking me to explain my heart, Kate. And I don't think I can put it into words. Oh, I can reel off any number of ways that you're special. I can tell you that I fall asleep at night thinking about you, that you warm my dreams, that when I'm standing in my bathroom shaving each morning I risk serious injury because I'm so anxious to get to work so I can see you. And then when I do . . . When I do see you, Katie, it's like every emotion inside me gets switched to high."

He stroked her cheek as if it were made of fine porcelain. "But nothing I've said begins to answer your question."

She felt a weird mixture of sorrow and elation. "You're wrong. It is a beginning, Brody. As much as I wish it weren't."

His hands moved over hers, which were still clasping her bra to her breasts. "Tell me your wishes, Katie."

Now her eyes misted over. "I don't think...anyone's ever really asked me that before," she whispered tremulously.

"Maybe no one else in your life has ever wanted to make your wishes come true as much as I do," he said, then kissed her, his eyes still open, as if he needed to confirm that she was really there, that she wouldn't vanish in a puff of his imagination.

As their lips parted, she said, "How could you be so sure I'd show up tonight?"

"I wasn't."

"But the candlelight, the fire, the wine. You do that every night?"

He grinned. "No. I just wanted to be prepared, in case. I wanted this desperately, Kate. And I knew that you did, too. But I didn't know if you'd allow yourself to reach deep enough inside."

She didn't quite understand what he meant.

"I knew you were scared."

She gave his words serious thought before speaking. "Of me more than you," she confessed. "Ever since I met you, I've been feeling a little like Alice falling down that rabbit hole, spinning out of control. And now," she said, her voice quivering, "here I am. In... Wonderland." Her hands dropped to her sides, letting her bra slip off her shoulders and flutter to the floor.

Brody gazed with awe at her full breasts, then cupped them in his hands like precious gifts. "Oh, yes, Katie. We're in Wonderland, all right."

She felt her heart racing. Her head truly was spinning—only the light-headedness felt good. "Hold me, Brody," she whispered. "Skin to skin."

He drew her into the circle of his arms, bringing her bare chest against his for the first time. "Not just skin to skin, darling," he murmured. "Heart to heart."

It was true, Kate thought, a tremor flashing through her like a lightning bolt. She could actually feel their heartbeats intermingling.

He held her close while time felt suspended. Even the tumult in her mind was stilled. The voice inside her head that had taunted her with warnings—*You mustn't do this. You can't do this. Stop before it's too late*—became mute as an all-encompassing languor and desire overtook her.

All Kate knew in those moments that connected them was that if Brody let go of her she would feel utterly bereft. And something else. Something she had riled against from the start. This wasn't merely lust she was feeling for Brody Baker. Or infatuation. This ran deeper. Seeped into her pores, flowed through her veins, made her feel alive and vibrant in a way that was altogether new for her. This feeling she could not yet dare to bring herself to name filled her with joy. And yet, even as she luxuriated in this newfound feeling, she knew despair was just around the corner.

"Brody, this isn't such a good idea," she said, even as she held on still tighter.

"We've gone beyond 'idea,' Katie," he replied huskily, running his palms along the length of her back, down over her jeans, and cupping her buttocks.

When he hoisted her up, her legs wrapped around his thighs as if there really was no other possible place for them.

His mouth moved to her breast and his tongue made contact with her nipple. Her head tilted back as she let out a little cry of pleasure.

He carried her over to the couch, and what she felt most at that moment was grateful that it was only a few steps away, now that desire and need had taken such a fierce hold on her.

He laid her on the couch and bent over her, tugging off her jeans and panties at the same time, removing her shoes along the way. He clearly knew exactly how to do this. How much practice had he had? How many women . . . ?

Brody was gazing down at her, quietly, intently. She felt shy and exposed, wishing that she hadn't quit going to the gym, wishing she'd resisted all those sweet rolls at the Full Moon. Would he find her wanting? This glorious Adonis. This "hunk" standing here, muscles rippling down his broad, tanned chest, his jeans open in a deep V—deep enough for her to see that he wasn't wearing any briefs beneath. For a moment she stopped worrying about her own body, basking in the glory of his. Until she caught him smiling down at her, his scrutiny nothing if not intense. Her self-consciousness returned with a vengeance.

She crossed her hands over her breasts, crossed her legs, tried to turn away from his intense study. At least there weren't any bright lights. The light from the hearth and the candles was as flattering as any lighting was ever going to be. No lights would have been better.

She shut her eyes. "I've got a thirty-five-year-old body, Brody. Replete with stretch marks and a scar from my cesarean section. Skye somehow managed to get the umbilical cord wrapped around her tiny neck. They had to go in quickly. The doc didn't do the neatest job of it."

A gasp escaped her lips as she felt the moist, warm tip of Brady's tongue tracing over the scar, his long hair falling like a fan across her stomach. The gesture was so tender and loving that tears slipped over Kate's eyelids. She remembered how much Arnie had hated that scar, had avoided ever touching it. And the few times she and Oscar had made love, he'd pretended it wasn't there. Come to think of it, he'd never actually seen it, since on the few occasions they'd made love, she'd opted for complete darkness, which had seemed fine with him. But then they'd operated from the start on never looking too closely at each other for fear of what they might see.

With Brody, there was no hiding. He had an inimitable way of forcing down all her defenses, peering behind all her barriers, physical and emotional. He demanded to see all there was to see.

She was scared. She had enough reasons, heaven knew, not to trust men, not to trust Brody, not to trust what she was feeling. Still, she had made her choice. She'd made it at the corner of Elm and South Ward. Whatever happened, this was where she'd chosen to be. *So,* she told herself, *stop worrying about tomorrow and just be happy tonight.*

Her resolve seemed to empower her, make her feel suddenly bold. She pulled Brody up to her, seeking out his mouth, kissing him deeply, greedily, covering his whole face with kisses, grasping his wild, long hair.

"Cover me, Brody. Cover me with your body."

He looked unsure for a moment. As if he couldn't believe this was all really happening. She saw a flush creep into his cheeks. For the first time, she sensed that he was a little nervous. To her surprise that touched her even more deeply than his obvious desire for her.

"Do you want some help with those jeans, Brody?"

Her offer made him smile. "That's awfully kind of you, ma'am, but I think I can manage," he drawled.

The jeans came off in one neat, swift movement.

A long, awed sigh escaped Kate's lips as she took in the ravishing sight of Brody Baker. *It should be a crime for any man to look this good,* she thought.

Heat flared through her whole body and she reached for him, pulling him down on top of her on the couch.

"I'll crush you," he said, as she bore his full weight.

"Yes, yes."

He nodded, his mouth closing over hers in a deep, fierce kiss that held a desperation that matched her own. The couch was narrow, leaving little room to maneuver, but it didn't matter. He pressed her into the cushions, his fingers digging into the soft skin of her thighs, her back arching up, their breathing growing ragged, their caresses becoming clumsy and wonderful.

She could feel him, hard and pulsating, as she drew her legs around him, opening herself to him, wanting to feel him inside her more than she'd ever wanted anything before. When he granted her wish, it was almost more than she could bear. She could hardly breathe. At the same time she was consumed by an agony of wanting more . . . more.

And then he was driving deeper and deeper inside her, her own thrusts adjusting to his quickening rhythm, matching his force. She heard cry after plaintive cry from a voice she didn't recognize as her own.

Her hair tangled with his, the sweat of their bodies intermingled. Tears stung her eyes. She felt as if she were breaking apart, shattering. Like Humpty Dumpty falling from the wall. All the king's horses and all the king's men would never be able to put her back together again.

Somehow it didn't matter. Nothing mattered but this ecstasy. She let herself fall. Toppling. Spinning. Defying gravity. . . .

November 7

My mom pulls up at the house just as I'm being dropped off by Alice's mom. It's ten o'clock. Made it home just in time. So, I see, did Mom. Boy, I'm thinking, she must have bought out the whole grocery store.

I give her a little wave. No big deal or anything. Or so I think until she practically springs out of the car, smiling from ear to ear, waving back at me. With both hands. Like she hasn't seen me for a year instead of a few hours.

So, right away I know something's up. If you're going to say one thing about my mom it would be that she's pretty predictable. Well, lately that hasn't been exactly the case. By lately I mean A.B.—after Brody. But this excessive cheeriness and high spirits, coming out of the blue like that—as Grandpa Leo says, I smell a little fishy here!

Then I see that she doesn't have any grocery bags with her. Hmm. And hmm again. Okay, I say to myself, maybe she went shopping earlier, dropped the stuff off at the house, then went out again. Maybe over to Aunt Rachel's or Aunt Julie's.

We meet up in the driveway and go into the house through the kitchen door and she's, like, chattering away. How was my practice? Isn't it cold outside?

How's Alice's mom? How's Alice? Did I score any goals? Mom, I tell her, it was *basketball* practice. You don't score *goals* in basketball. Oh, right, she says with a little giggle. Basketball. Hoops. You score hoops. Baskets, I tell her. We score baskets. Right, she says. Baskets. Did I score any baskets?

By now we're in the kitchen and I'm looking around. Like, where are the groceries? I kind of nonchalantly stroll over to the fridge—the grocery list is still stuck to the door with a What I Make Best Is Reservations magnet—and open it. The shelves are as empty as they were before we left for my practice.

Whatever she's been doing for the past three hours, it obviously *did not* include buying groceries.

Meanwhile, Mom's still in overdrive, bustling around the kitchen, snatching dishes from the drainboard and putting them away, wiping down the counters. This is not, I repeat, *typical Mom*. Not that she's a slob or anything, but kitchen cleanup, especially at ten at night, is not something she usually gets up for. I drum my fingers on the fridge door.

"Mom, I thought you were going to the grocery store."

She keeps on wiping even though there's not so much as a crumb on the counter. "Oh, I did," she says, not looking over at me. "I went all the way to Louden. I could have gone to Cobb's, but no, I figured since I wanted to get a lot of stuff and I had so much time, I'd drive over to Louden. Cobb's does have better meat, but there's a much better selection of fruits and vegetables and stuff.... Anyway, you won't believe this."

And I'm thinking to myself, *You're probably right*, but I don't say a word.

"The dumbest thing," she says, and she's still got her back to me. "I got all the way over there and I even managed to grab up the last cart and then, wouldn't you know it, I realized I didn't have my shopping list."

I start to ask her why she didn't just drive on home and get it. After all, she had three whole hours—plenty enough time to go back and forth from Louden twice over and still get all her shopping done.

And then I notice that her sweatshirt's on *backward!*

8

THE GLOW KATE WAS feeling lasted until about two in the morning and then the guilt hit. Like a thunderbolt. She sat up in bed in a sweat, her heart thumping, only this time her condition had nothing to do with feeling aroused.

She pressed her clammy palms to her cheeks. *What have I done?*

Okay, she knew what she'd done. The question quickly became *Why did I do it?*

Who was she kidding? She knew why she'd done it. Brody Baker had managed, in short order, to turn a switch on inside her that even she hadn't known existed. A high-voltage, crackling, sizzling switch.

Her cheeks blazed as she thought about just how brazen and wanton she'd been with Brody. Had that really been her? With Arnie, and those few times with Oscar, she'd always been so restrained when it came to making love; always holding back a little, never fully trusting; never feeling it was safe to let go. With Brody, not only had she held nothing back, she'd given expression to a passion that only he had been able to ignite.

It was this very passion she was now desperately trying to extinguish. Even as she chastised herself and began listing all of the reasons why it had to end right then and there, she found herself picturing Brody's naked body, the two of them entwined in each other's arms, twisting, arching, kissing, coming together in a frenzy with long, slick thrusts. . . .

Stop! her head shouted. *Don't think about it.* But it was no use. Brody Baker had thrust his way into her mind with as much fire and determination as he'd thrust his way into her body. The only real question was how to exorcise him.

She ended up spending the rest of the night trying her best to do just that. All that resulted was that she didn't get a wink of sleep.

BLEARY-EYED, KATE poured herself a cup of coffee in her kitchen the next morning, while she debated whether or not to cancel the staff meeting that was scheduled for ten o'clock. Her attempts at exorcism having failed miserably, she wasn't feeling at all ready to face Brody. And the idea of facing him and everyone else at the station at the same time was really more than she could handle. Still, what excuse could she give? And how could she have spent so many hours the night before, reminding herself that she had to put all of her focus and attention on running WPIT instead of on WPIT's program director, and then, the first thing the next morning, be thinking about negating her responsibilities? Thanks to Brody, there were a lot of changes going on at the station. To his credit, he'd infused new energy into the whole staff and everyone was so gung ho. This forward momentum was something Kate knew she had to capitalize on. Now, if only she could stop thinking about the altogether different kind of energy and momentum Brody Baker had infused in her.

At close to eight, Skye, dressed in worn blue jeans and an oversize rugby shirt, black high-top sneakers still in hand, came bursting into the kitchen in a rush to gobble down some breakfast and get to school. She skidded to a stop when she saw her mother sitting at the table and gave her a startled look.

"You're in your bathrobe."

"Is there something wrong with my bathrobe?" Kate asked defensively. With so many worries on her mind, she'd forgotten she hadn't even gotten dressed for work yet.

Skye scowled. "No. It's just that usually you're dressed, gulping down coffee and running out the door by this time," she said, kneeling to put on her sneakers. "Aren't you going to work today?"

Kate affected a casual shrug. "Of course, I am. I'm just a little slow getting started this morning, that's all."

A real contrast from the night before, Skye mused, when her mother had been a regular fireball.

"Are you sick, Mom?"

I'm sick, all right, Kate thought. *Sick at heart. Nothing like throwing yourself at a man and behaving like a complete hussy to bring on what's ailing me.*

The feel of her daughter's cool hand on her forehead brought Kate back to the present tense. "I'm fine, Skye."

"I don't know, Mom. You feel a little feverish to me."

Feverish. If Skye only knew the half of it. *Thank God, she doesn't,* Kate thought.

She glanced at Skye. Why was her daughter looking at her so strangely? Did she suspect something? Were there any telltale signs?

No, Kate assured herself. That was ridiculous. Skye couldn't have the faintest clue where she'd spent last evening.

Then again, Skye had a very vivid imagination. And, after all, she hadn't said a word about where she'd been from seven to ten the night before. And there was no way her daughter would have missed noticing that there was no more food in the house this morning than there had been last night before she'd gone grocery shopping. *Allegedly* gone grocery shopping.

Kate felt a rush of panic. She had to give Skye some sort of explanation. Her first thought was to simply say that she'd gone over to one of her sisters' houses and the time flew by and she never got to the market. A plausible excuse, only it meant that she'd have to get either Julie or Rachel to back her up, which would mean they'd start asking questions, and she'd either have to try lying to them or tell them the truth. She felt like she was trapped between a rock and a hard place. She hated weaving lie upon lie. Besides, her sisters were sure to see through her. And if she told them the truth... No, that wouldn't do. Julie and Rachel were already in Brody's corner. They'd really get on her case if they knew she'd... had one weak moment. Even though she was determined not to have another.

Nervously, Kate grabbed a box of Sugar Crackle cereal from the cupboard shelf and began pouring some into a bowl for Skye. As she brought the bowl over to the table, she said in as offhand a way as she could, "You'll never guess who I bumped into last night in...in Louden."

Skye hid a smile. Her mother usually banned sugary cereals for breakfast. She was not, however, going to question her good fortune. As her Grandpa Leo would say, never look a gift horse in the mouth.

"I mean," Kate went on, crossing to the refrigerator and taking out the container of milk, "you were probably wondering where I...what I...how come I...got home so late."

"I figured you must have bumped into someone," Skye said airily.

"Exactly," Kate was quick to agree. And repeat. "Exactly." She poured milk into Skye's cereal bowl, and the little sugary nuggets floated to the top.

"It was an old friend," Kate said, as she kept pouring the milk into the bowl to the point where those sugary nuggets were threatening to jump overboard. Skye tipped the container back in the nick of time.

Kate absently set the milk down on the table. "An old school friend."

"From Pittsville High?" Skye asked, deadpan.

No, Kate thought. It couldn't be anyone local. Too easy for Skye to check and catch her in a lie.

A lie. Guilt flooded her. Now she was lying to her daughter—the child she'd raised to be truthful, always trying to set a good example herself. This was getting worse and worse. Only what alternative did she have? She certainly couldn't tell Skye the truth. *Oh, darling, guess where I was last night. At Brody's place, making wild, passionate love with him.*

"Actually a gal I used to be pretty friendly with in college. Well, not really all that friendly, but I certainly... liked her. She was very nice and we had a few classes together...."

Kate bit down on her bottom lip. *That's right. Don't just stand there making up a lie to your only child—elaborate on the lie. Why dig a hole when you can dig a grave?*

"So I guess I never could have guessed who you bumped into, then."

"What?"

"Since I never have met any of your college friends and I don't even remember you ever having mentioned anyone in particular."

"Oh. Well . . . that's true. It was just a . . . figure of speech. You know. You'll never guess. . . ." She flashed a sham smile.

Skye smiled back. Boy, she thought, her mom had to be the world's worst liar. Still, if it made her feel better . . .

"What was her name?"

"Her name?"

"Your sort of college friend," Skye asked just before she slipped a large spoonful of milky Sugar Crackles into her mouth.

"Amanda. Mandy. We called her Mandy. Or Man. Well, really, hardly anyone ever called her that, now that I think of it." Kate took in a gulp of air. "She was passing through."

Skye swallowed another spoonful of cereal. "Passing through?"

Kate could feel her pulse beating in her ears. She not only hated lying, she was lousy at it. Still, Skye seemed to be buying the story. "Through Louden. I bumped into her in the . . . parking lot and we . . . went for coffee. The time just . . . slipped by so fast. Because we were both . . . talking so much. You know, sharing old times. That sort of thing."

"Hmm."

Kate warily eyed her daughter. Maybe Skye wasn't buying her tall tale. "Tall tale" somehow sounded better than "lie." "What does that mean?"

"What does what mean, Mom?"

"Hmm." Kate imitated her daughter's inflection.

Skye shrugged. "Hmm doesn't mean anything. It just means . . .oh."

"Oh, what?"

"Oh, that's . . . nice. I'm glad you had so much fun," Skye said, about to swallow another spoonful of cereal.

"I didn't say I had *so much* fun. We just . . . talked and. . .stuff. No big deal or anything. I'll probably never see her again. I'm actually quite positive I won't. Like I said, she was passing through. It was just a . . . a one-time thing." At least that much wasn't a lie.

Skye looked across at her mother. "Are you sure you're okay, Mom? You look kind of flushed. And your eyes are a little bloodshot."

Kate's hands flew to her cheeks. They did feel hot. And of course, her eyes were bloodshot. She hadn't slept a wink. "Maybe. . .maybe I am coming down with something." She was coming down with *something,* all right. And that something was Brody Baker.

The phone rang. Saved by the bell, Kate thought, breathing an inward sigh of relief.

"It's probably Alice wanting to make sure she didn't forget to do some homework assignment," Skye said, making a dash for the phone. "I'll bet she forgot to do math. Now she'll have to make up a story for Mrs. Waters. Alice can tell some real whoppers."

Kate felt consumed with guilt as she watched Skye lift the receiver off the wall phone on the other side of the kitchen.

"Oh, hi," she said brightly. "Yeah, she's right here. . . . Sure, hold on a sec." Skye extended the receiver in Kate's direction. "It's for you, Mom."

Kate started across the room to answer it.

"It's Brody," Skye said blandly.

Kate came to an abrupt stop. Then her gaze locked with Skye's. Her daughter's tone might have been innocuous, but was that a sparkle Kate spied in those young, innocent green eyes? Was Skye on to her?

"Mom? He's waiting."

Kate stayed rooted to the spot. She couldn't talk to Brody now. She simply couldn't. She made an abrupt detour to the kitchen table, scooping up Skye's unfinished bowl of cereal from the place mat, and started carrying it over to the sink. "Oh, could you . . . tell him that I'm running behind schedule. I'll...call him back. Better still, I'll just . . . see him at work."

Skye dashed over to the sink, rescuing her cereal in the nick of time. "I haven't finished yet. And Brody says it's important. I really think you should take it, Mom."

Kate shot a look at the dangling receiver. What she wanted to do was walk right over there and drop it back in its cradle. If she did that, though, what would Skye think?

All of this thinking about what her daughter would think was giving Kate a terrible headache.

Reluctantly she crossed the room and picked up the receiver like she was grabbing a battering ram. "Yes? What is it?" she asked sharply.

"Don't tell me," Brody drawled. "You got no more sleep than I did, last night."

True enough, Kate thought, although she was sure from the sound of Brody's voice that their reasons for lack of sleep were worlds apart. "I'm running late. I don't have time to talk now. I haven't even taken my shower and . . ." Sheer embarrassment made her let the rest of the sentence fall off. Last night, before she'd left Brody's place, they'd showered together. And made love under the hot, steamy spray. She remembered how she'd gasped, his name catching in her throat, when he'd pressed her against the cold shower tiles. She remembered the chill and the heat, as his seductive mouth and hands laid claim to every inch of her. . . .

Embarrassment gave way to arousal. She turned her back to Skye. Her cheeks were blazing; her body ached.

"I won't keep you," Brody murmured over the wire. "Not that I wouldn't have liked to keep you last night, Katie. I keep thinking what it would be like waking up beside you, reaching for you in the early-morning light. Have you ever made love at the crack of dawn?"

Kate could feel Skye's eyes boring into her even though her back was turned to her daughter. "I really think we should . . . discuss this at work," she said, nervously twining the coiled telephone cord around her index finger.

"Before or after the staff meeting?" he asked in that teasing, lighthearted tone that had driven her to distraction only last night.

She paced back and forth as far as the coiled cord would take her. "I really have to . . ."

"I know. You have to take a shower. It won't be the same without me there to scrub your back."

Oh, those magical fingers gliding up and down her soapy spine. The memory was so tangible it felt like a wonderfully sweet taste in her mouth. And then Kate inadvertently glanced at Skye, who was giving her an assessing look.

The taste in Kate's mouth instantly turned sour. She hung up without another word.

"I'm going to . . . get dressed." She turned and glanced back at her daughter as she got to the door, in time to see her downing the last of her Sugar Crackle. "Really,

Skye, you should eat something more...nourishing for breakfast."

As Kate disappeared through the swing door, Skye sat there wearing a Cheshire-cat smile.

IT WAS HALF PAST NINE when Kate got to work. With a firm resolve, she strode directly down the hall to Brody's office. She had to put him straight. What had happened last night was a disaster in the making. The only solution was to put an end to it before things blew up in both their faces.

Not bothering to knock, she threw his door open. "Brody, I need to speak to you."

"Kate..."

"No, let me do the talking. I have to explain about last night." She started to close the door behind her, her eyes fixed on Brody. "I'm afraid you're getting the wrong—" Her mouth fell open. Only as the door shut did she realize someone was standing just to the side of it. Carl Dermott. Pittsville High's basketball coach.

Kate's complexion went chalky.

Carl Dermott, a bear of a man in his early thirties, gave Kate a big-toothed smile. "Hey, talk about timing."

Kate blinked several times in confusion.

"I was just telling Carl that he had great comic timing," Brody explained with a smile.

Kate's expression bore a mix of confusion and embarrassment as her gaze shifted from Carl to Brody. What was her program director cooking up now? She didn't have to wait long for an answer.

"Brody, here, thinks I could head up a comedy spot after the late-night news on Friday nights," Carl told her. "I'd have to get some new material, natch, but heck, that's easy enough. Like Brody says, it's all in the rhythm and the timing. You remember how I brought the house down at the PTA annual picnic in June, Kate. Bernie Hutchins played bluegrass on his banjo and got a pretty good hand, but then I came on and did a good ten-minute schtick and had you all rolling in the aisles. Well, on the grass. Remember, Kate?"

At the moment, she would have been hard put to remember her own name.

"Wait, wait," Carl said with a wave of his hand. "This'll bring it back. This was one of my best. See, there's this real cute little tike, Tommy, who goes up to this lifeguard at the beach. He kinda tugs on the lifeguard's swim trunks and the lifeguard looks down at him. 'What can I do for you, son?' the lifeguard asks him, real friendly like. And the tike points to the ocean and asks, 'Can I swim in the sea?' The lifeguard ruffles his hair. 'Sure you can, son.' And the tike says, 'Gee, that's funny. In my swimming pool at home I can't swim a stroke.'"

Carl was clearly waiting for the laughs. Brody obliged with a little chuckle. Kate was too distracted and overwrought to crack so much as a smile.

"Well, naturally," Carl said, looking a little disappointed, "that one's for the kiddos more than the grown-ups. There were lots of kids at that picnic and you gotta gear your material to your audience. Certainly for a late-night spot, I could get a little . . ." He paused to wink at them both. "Well, you know. Nothing real off-color or anything. That's not my kind of thing, any which way. No sirree. I've got my reputation in the community to think about." As he said the last sentence, the coach's eyes strayed in Kate's direction, then quickly skidded away.

Brody ambled over to Carl and put a friendly arm around his shoulders. "Like I said right off the bat, coach, I have to get Kate's approval before we move ahead. If it's a go, I'll let you know and we'll work on the material together."

"Right. Sure," Carl said, letting Brody guide him in the direction of the door. "And don't forget about Cindy. She's a real card. Cracks me up." He looked over at Kate. "Cindy Towers. You know her, Kate. She moved down here about a year ago. The pretty, little brunette dental hygienist that works for Doc Lowell over on Market Street. Is she funny or is she funny?"

"I . . . don't really know her," Kate muttered.

"You've got to audition her, Brody," Carl said emphatically. "I kid you not that she'll have you in stitches. And like you said, you want to have at least three comics for each half-hour segment, with a pool of about twelve so that you can rotate us. . . ."

Brody had the coach right to the door. He reached for the knob.

Carl's hand shot up. "I got one more for you. Why is it folks carry umbrellas?" He looked expectantly from Brody to Kate, then back to Brody again.

"Gee, Carl, I don't know," Brody said. "Because it's raining."

"Naw," the coach said with a broad grin. "Because umbrellas can't walk."

"Very funny," Brody said, easing Carl out the door. "I'll be in touch."

Carl ambled out. "Don't worry about me running dry. I've got plenty more where those came from."

Brody shut the door, grinning. "I'm sure he has."

His grin was replaced by a questioning smile as he turned to Kate. "Okay, he's low on originality, but you've got to admit, his timing's . . ."

"It's not his timing that I'm thinking about," Kate said morosely. "It's mine. It's lousy. Has been for . . . a while now."

"I couldn't disagree more, Katie. I think your timing was great last night."

He started toward her, but she raised a hand. "Stop right there. Last night was a big mistake, Brody. I don't know what came over me. I think maybe I'm getting the flu or something. I've been feeling quite light-headed lately. Not at all myself."

"Not at all yourself?" Brody echoed.

She squared her shoulders. "I'm a very reserved person."

He grinned. "You give the word *reserve* a whole new meaning, Katie."

She threw her hands up in the air. "See? That's what I mean."

"What do you mean?"

"I'm trying to explain, damn it. I haven't been myself these past few weeks. This is not me," she said, slapping her chest in dismay.

"Then who is this ravishing woman standing before me?" Brody teased. "Who was that warm, vital, uninhibited beauty I was making love with last night?"

Kate had no answer. She looked away.

He came up to her. "This is you, Katie. It's the you that you've kept locked away for years and years."

"I really don't want to talk about this anymore, Brody. We have a staff meeting in—" she shot a look at her watch "—twenty minutes. I need to . . . I have to . . ."

"This is what you need, Katie. This is what you have to do."

The next thing she knew she was in his arms. Her lips moved in protest, but no sound emerged. She felt the spread of his large hands on her back. She looked up into his eyes, which were as blue as cornflowers. His mouth was but a breath away. A kiss away.

"Only you have to admit it first, Katie."

She could feel her resolve start to crumble. Oh, how she wanted that kiss. Her chest felt tight and her heart was thumping so hard against her chest that it hurt. At the last moment, reason prevailed.

Her hands went up to his chest. "I can't, Brody. I can't have an . . . affair with you. I tried that once and it was a disaster. This is a small town. I have a fourteen-year-old daughter to think about. I have a position of responsibility. A lot of people who rely on me." She sighed wearily. "I'm too old for this." Right now she felt as old as Methuselah.

"That's not what this is about, Kate."

"I don't expect you to understand."

"I understand more than you do."

"That's not true. . . ."

"You're scared. You're scared that I'm going to hurt you like Arnie. Like Oscar."

"I'm already. . . hurting," she confessed. "This morning I lied to my daughter. I hate myself for doing it."

He released her, letting his hands drop to his sides. "And you blame me."

She shook her head. "No. I chose to go to your place last night. I think, deep down, I was hoping that—"

"Nothing would happen?"

"Oh, I knew something would happen. I was just hoping it wouldn't be . . . that good. So I could leave, telling myself that I'd gotten the whole thing out of my system. I'd see this for what it was."

"And what's that?"

"A ridiculous infatuation."

His blue eyes blazed. "And is that what you saw? Is that what you see right this minute when you look at me, Katie?"

She couldn't look at him. "I made a fool of myself one time too many, Brody. Do you know what it's like having everyone in town feeling sorry for you, no doubt thinking you're as big an idiot as you think you are yourself? I'm not going through that again. I can't handle it."

He cupped her chin, forcing her to face him. "No woman's going to show up at your door claiming to be my wife, Kate. Because there is no wife. No wife, no kid, no girlfriend. Sure, I've had my share of relationships, but I've never been serious about anyone before. Not like I'm serious about you. Remember that first day? When I told you it was chemistry?"

She nodded slowly. "I remember."

"Well, it's more than chemistry, Katie. We're two halves of one whole. We fit together perfectly. I'm not just talking sex, but while we're on that subject, the sex was great. The best. It was like what you always hoped it would be, only in real life it somehow never quite hit the mark. Do you know what I mean?"

She knew only too well.

Brody smiled like he knew she knew. "Until last night. Last night it was a bull's-eye."

She could feel her cheeks start to glow. "Look what you've reduced me to," she scolded. "A blushing adolescent. Don't do this, Brody. It isn't fair. I don't want to get involved with you. It's too complicated. I've got too many other things on my mind. I don't have the time. Or the energy."

"Wanna bet I can recharge your batteries?" he teased, playfully skimming his hand down the front of her blouse.

She slapped his hand away. "Will you behave yourself? We have a staff meeting."

He smiled sheepishly. "I'd better not sit next to you, then. I don't know if I'll be able to control myself."

She turned on her heel. "Oh, really, Brody. You're impossible."

"Hey."

She stopped at the door and glanced back at him. "What?"

"How about tonight?"

"No. Positively no."

"I'm making barbecued ribs. They're Skye's favorite."

"Forget it. I am not going back to your place. With or without my daughter."

"Fine. If you won't come to the barbecue, the barbecue will simply have to come to you. I'll be over, say, around seven-thirty."

She turned away and opened the door. "I won't be home."

"Scaredy-cat."

"You are such a—" Kate stopped. Julie and Ben were out in the hall. They both grinned at her. She frowned. "He wants to start a stand-up comedy show after the eleven o'clock news on Friday nights," she muttered to the pair. "I was just telling him I didn't think it was such a . . . good idea."

Brody popped his head out the door. "She thinks it's a perfectly good idea. She's nuts about a lot of my ideas. They just make her a little nervous, that's all."

Julie smiled. "I like the idea of a comedy show. Who couldn't use a few laughs now and then? Especially after the late-night news."

"Well, I'm sure Coach Dermott will have you rolling in the aisles," Kate said sardonically.

"Carl?" Ben queried.

"He just needs a little polishing," Brody said, stepping out into the hall. "He actually told a cute joke about this little kid—"

Kate raised a hand to silence him. "Please. Once was quite enough, thank you."

Brody grinned at her. "You don't really mean that."

Kate glared at him, then stormed ahead of the threesome.

Julie and Ben glanced quizzically over at Brody.

"What gives with her?" Julie asked.

Brody smiled. "I think she woke up on the wrong side of the bed."

Ben grinned. "Or maybe it was the wrong bed."

Julie gave her husband a little poke, but she was grinning, too.

IT WAS ALMOST SIX WHEN Kate got home that night. Skye was in the kitchen working on some math problems. She greeted her mother with a little grunt as she attacked her calculator.

Kate kept her coat on, her key chain dangling from her finger. "Hey, how about going out for a pizza tonight? Or Chinese?"

"Can't."

Kate frowned. "Too much homework?"

Skye looked up. "No, silly. Brody's coming over with barbecued ribs. He said you might forget."

"How did you . . . I mean, when did you find out—"

"Oh, he called about an hour ago to remind me to remind you." Skye scribbled down the numbers on her calculator. "There. Last problem done."

Kate was seething. The nerve of the man. So Brody thought he had a foolproof plan, did he?

"Well, I'll just call him up and tell him that we already have plans," Kate said firmly, striding toward the phone.

"We don't already have plans, Mom."

"We have plans to . . . to have a quiet night at home. This is a school night."

"I have to eat on school nights, too. And you know how I love barbecued ribs."

Kate began pacing, her coat still on, the keys still jangling from her finger. "It's just not . . . convenient. Not tonight."

Skye closed her math book and focused her attention fully on her mother. "What's wrong, Mom? Don't you want to see Brody?"

"No. I mean, no, it's not that. It's just that I'm not in the mood for . . . company tonight. I'm beat."

"Then it's perfect that Brody's coming over. You won't have to go dragging off to some crowded restaurant—"

"I'm sure it won't be crowded at the Panda . . ."

"And you won't have to cook." Skye gave her mother an assessing look. "You might want to change, though. What about a pair of jeans and that neat-looking peach turtleneck sweater that you hardly ever wear?"

"I hardly ever wear it because it's too snug."

"Come on, Mom. You look dynamite in that sweater."

"I have absolutely no interest in looking dynamite."

Skye rolled her eyes as she gathered up her books. "And they say teenagers are hard to figure out."

"BECAUSE UMBRELLAS can't walk."

Skye broke into a peel of laughter. "Oh, Brody, that's the worst joke I've ever heard."

Kate arched a brow. "Then why are you laughing?"

"It's the way Brody tells it. You should go on the show yourself," Skye told him, as the threesome sat around the kitchen table at Kate's house. Despite Kate's protests, Skye had set the table with a white linen tablecloth and festive red linen napkins. She'd even switched the plain everyday drinking glasses for the rarely used crystal water goblets.

"Naw, I'm better behind the scenes," he said with a smile at Kate.

"Skye, are you finished with your ribs?" Kate asked abruptly. "Because if you are, we really should clean up here and let Brody go on home. We've all had a long day. Besides, you still need to get some homework done."

"I finished my homework."

"And I—"

"Have to take a shower?" Brody asked with a teasing wink.

"I have to clean up the kitchen and then I've got a lot of paperwork to tackle," she said severely.

"I tell you what," Skye said, standing. "I'll do the cleanup and put on some coffee. You two go on into the living room and just . . . relax."

"Skye, I—" Kate started to protest.

"How do you take your coffee, Brody?" Skye interrupted.

"I like it sweet. Two sugars, a little milk."

"Mom?"

"Black. And only half a cup. You can make instant."

Brody rose and came up behind Kate's chair. "May I?"

She gave him a narrow look. *No, you may not,* she thought, but said, "Thank you," very formally, as he pulled her chair out for her.

When they got to the living room, Brody sat down on the couch and Kate deliberately chose the armchair that put her farthest away from him.

"Sorry about the ribs," he said.

"What do you mean?"

"Well, you hardly touched them."

"They were fine. I just wasn't very hungry."

They lapsed into silence. Kate folded her hands in her lap, and studied them. Brody studied Kate.

"She's a great kid."

Kate looked over at him. "I guess it's pretty mutual. She thinks you're the funniest guy around, the best cook, the . . . best looking."

"What does her mom think?"

"Her mom thinks—" She stopped, noticing that the lights had dimmed.

Brody grinned. "I saw a hand sneak around the corner to the dimmer switch."

"Really, that child." She frowned at Brody. "This is all your fault."

Brody slid over to the other side of the couch, closer to her. "My fault?"

"Oh, don't play innocent with me. You get her to tell you my favorite flower, my favorite poet, my favorite color. Heaven only knows what else you pried out of her about me. Then you go and make her favorite food so you'll please her, getting her to think that if she's pleased, I'll be pleased."

"The point being?" Brody asked.

"Don't start playing Mr. Innocent now. You see how she's behaving. It's obvious she thinks you've got a crush on me."

He grinned. "I do have a crush on you, Katie."

"Well, I'd just as soon she didn't know about it. Especially as I'm trying my best to . . . to put an end to it."

"Your lips may say no, no, but your eyes are saying something else altogether."

"I'm trying to be serious here, Brody," she scolded.

"I like you better when you're not so serious."

"Well, this is the real me. I view things in a very serious light."

"The wrong things."

"See? We don't see eye-to-eye on anything. We're complete opposites."

"Katie, relax. Stop trying so hard."

"Trying what?"

His blue-eyed gaze fixed on her face. "To drive me off."

"Brody..."

Skye arrived with two mugs of steaming hot, freshly brewed coffee. "Gee, Brody, I'd have thought you'd have a fire going by now."

Brody grinned. "Well, it's not too late."

"Yes, it is," Kate said. "Anyway, we...we don't have any logs."

"Sure we do, Mom," Skye said, deliberately setting both mugs next to each other on the coffee table in front of the sofa. "A big pile of them, stacked up in the garage. I'll go get some. And then I'd better go upstairs and do the rest of my homework."

"I thought you told me you'd finished your homework," Kate said.

"Well, the regular assignments, but there are a bunch that I could do for extra credit. You're the one always telling me, 'Don't do the least you can do, do the most.' I'm just taking your advice," Skye said with a bright smile.

Kate had to smile herself as Skye took off. "I think my real daughter must have been captured by aliens and they set this remarkable lookalike down here in her place."

"See what a good influence I am on her? You should have me over more often," Brody said, going over to the fireplace and using some kindling stacked in a wicker basket beside the hearth to get a fire started. A minute later, Skye bounded back with enough logs to keep the fire going for several hours. After dumping them beside Brody, she bid them both a cheery goodnight, making a big point of saying she wouldn't bother to come down again before going to bed.

After Brody got the fire roaring, he sat back down on the couch, patting the cushion beside him.

"Come on over here and have your coffee. I promise I won't bite."

She hesitated, then joined him. "You really have to leave after we've had our coffee, Brody. I'm worn-out."

He smiled. "I'm still running on that adrenaline rush that hit me the moment I saw you at my door last night."

"I wish we could forget it ever happened."

"I couldn't even if I wanted to," he said quietly. "And I don't want to, Katie."

Cupping his mug with both hands, Brody leaned his head back against the couch and closed his eyes. Kate looked over at him. There was such warmth and contentment on his handsome face.

Kate felt an almost-irresistible impulse to lean over and kiss him. Without her realising it, her head began inching in his direction.

"Are you ready to admit it, Katie?" Brody murmured, his eyes still closed.

She spied the teasing curve of his mouth and sighed. He was a heartbreaker, no doubt about it. She sure could pick them. No one's fault but her own that she always ended up getting hurt in the end.

Brody opened his eyes slowly, gazing at her face. And she knew it was no use pretending. He really could see right into her.

"I admit it." The words were hers, but somehow they sounded as if they belonged to someone else. But as his mouth moved over hers, claiming it, it felt so good, so right. *This,* she thought, *belongs to me.*

9

KATE WOKE UP LATE the next morning and didn't get to the station until nine, an hour later than usual. She snatched up the pile of mail and folders from the in tray on Kelly's desk, giving her secretary a rushed smile of greeting as she headed for her office. "I've got a ton of work to do today."

"You've got . . . company," Kelly said, just as Kate started to open the door to her office. A whisper of a smile played on Kate's lips. She had a good idea who that "company" was.

She was wrong.

"Agnes." The instant Kate saw her ex-mother-in-law sitting primly on one of the straight-back chairs, she came to an abrupt stop, her smile vanishing in a flash.

"There was a time," Agnes said archly, "when work around here began promptly at eight."

Kate stiffened. It was a totally unfair reprimand, not to mention that it was none of Agnes Pilcher's business what time she showed up for work.

Kate drew her shoulders back as she marched over to her desk and sat down, regarding her ex-mother-in-law with an impatient look. "Is there something you wanted, Agnes?"

The thin-faced woman, with her beakish nose and frown lines that dug into the corners of her mouth, returned an imperious gaze. "Skye dropped by my house after school yesterday. Did she tell you?"

Kate was too taken aback by this news to remember to hide the look of surprise from her face. Skye hadn't said a word to her about it. Not to mention that her daughter rarely visited her grandmother these days without first receiving an invitation, and then she only went reluctantly. Oh, Skye was polite and respectful to her grandmother and, for her part, Agnes did show genuine affection for her granddaughter, inasmuch as she was capable of showing it. Yet their get-togethers tended to be rather formal and strained. Invariably, they sat together in Agnes's stuffy Victorian parlor where Agnes would serve Skye tea—which Skye detested except when she was sick, and then only with sugar, a substance that her grandmother refused to have in her home—and dry, homemade biscuits served with orange marmalade. Skye hated orange marmalade even more than she hated tea without sugar. Fortunately, those meetings rarely lasted more than an hour and Skye always treated her grandmother's dismissals as reprieves. So what was Skye doing, dropping over there of her own free will?

"Well, that was nice for . . . both of you," Kate said cautiously. "Did you have a pleasant visit?"

Agnes was not one for chitchat. Especially with her son's ex-wife. She came right to the point. "Skye seems to think you're about to remarry."

Kate's mouth dropped open. "What?"

"There's certainly enough gossip around town about you and Mr. Baker. Really, Kate. First that no-account scoundrel this summer, and now this . . . this hippie. Rumors are flying."

Kate could feel her cheeks grow hot. "I have better things to do with my time than to listen to rumors."

Right. Like making passionate love with the very man everyone was gossiping about.

Agnes regarded Kate with true disdain. "She was particularly concerned about your divorce decree."

"I . . . I don't understand."

"Don't you? Are you trying to tell me you didn't tell your daughter that, because of her father, you could never remarry?"

Kate was truly flabbergasted. "Of course not. What would ever give Skye such a notion?"

"She is well aware that you are a woman who wants to have her cake and eat it, too." Each of Agnes's words was spoken as if it was being sliced out with a sharp knife.

Kate stared at Agnes. The light was beginning to dawn. "Are you telling me that Skye knows about my arrangement with Arnie concerning WPIT?"

"Really, Kate, I'd have thought you wouldn't use your own daughter to try to do your bidding for you," Agnes reprimanded.

Kate sprang up from her seat. She was boiling mad. "That's quite enough, Agnes. I don't know how Skye found out the details of my divorce decree with Arnie. I certainly didn't tell her. Simply because there was no reason to tell her. You see, I have absolutely no intention of remarrying. Skye merely has an overactive imagination. She obviously gets it from the Pilcher side of the family!"

Agnes folded her hands primly in her lap, unperturbed by Kate's outburst. "I know you think that I'd like nothing more than to see you get married again, Kate, just so WPIT would once again be in my son's hands. Which I assure you it would, so you can stop using your daughter to try to get me to persuade Arnie otherwise—"

"I told you that I did not—"

Agnes waved off the rest of Kate's rebuttal. "And while I have never hidden my displeasure with the changes you've been making here at the station, nor with your choice of new...personnel, if regaining control of WPIT means you marrying Mr. Brody Baker, I'd just as soon continue to watch the station go down the tubes."

Kate was momentarily at a loss for which of Agnes's unjustified accusations to attack first. She went with Brody since he was foremost on her mind at the moment. "And just what have you got against Brody Baker?" she demanded.

Agnes's head tilted in a hawklike fashion. "I don't think he is a suitable stepfather for my granddaughter."

Kate clenched her hands into tight little fists. The nerve of the woman. As if Agnes's lying, cheat of a son had proved to be a shining example of fatherhood.

"What is it, Agnes? The long hair? The motorcycle? The way he dresses?"

Agnes sneered. "I'll grant you I find his appearance off-putting, but not nearly so much as—"

"As what?" Kate interrupted, getting really revved up now. "The fact that he has some innovative ideas? That he's bringing WPIT out of the Dark Ages? That he's—"

"That he's an ex-convict," Agnes declared, regarding her ex-daughter-in-law with thinly veiled disdain.

Kate's mouth was open but no words came out. She felt like she'd just been sucker punched. Could she possibly have heard right? Had Agnes just stated that Brody was an *ex-convict?* No. No, it wasn't possible.

"I take it from your expression that Mr. Baker failed to list that particular residence on his résumé and, thus, this comes as a surprise to you, Kate," Agnes said with no hint of sympathy. Quite the opposite. She looked to be gloating. Clearly, this announcement had made her day.

"Yet another example of how you run things around here. Hiring a man without doing a thorough background check... When I was in charge of hiring, I certainly didn't employ someone based on his... sex appeal." Agnes said *sex appeal* like they were dirty words. Not to mention that her attack was wholly unjustified. If anything, Brody's admitted sex appeal had worked strongly against him. The only reason Kate had hired him was because of his obvious talent as a program director. And she had taken him on for a probationary period, besides. All of that, however, seemed irrelevant in the wake of this new, mind-boggling revelation.

"I don't believe you," Kate said, her voice strained, her throat as dry as sandpaper.

"Then I leave it to you to check with the San Padres County Jail in San Padres, Texas, as I did. I believe you will find that your Mr. Baker resided there for a period of nearly one year or thereabouts," Agnes said, with a wave of her hand.

Kate clasped her hands together on her desk simply because they had begun to tremble. A year? In prison? Brody?

She tried desperately not to let Agnes see how badly shaken she was. "What... did he do?" she asked in a tight, controlled voice.

"The charge," the older woman said solemnly, "was simple assault, although, personally, I don't think something as violent as assault can ever be simple. I don't know the details, but I imagine Mr. Baker can provide some. If you can believe what he says. And if the details really matter," she added, smoothing down her drab gray wool skirt.

Stunned, Kate just sat there. Assault? Could the same man who had been so tender and gentle those past two evenings they'd spent together have actually spent time in prison for beating someone up? She told herself Agnes had got it wrong. It must have been a different Brody Baker. It couldn't be her Brody Baker.

Her Brody Baker. One night of passion, a cozy evening in front of her hearth, and already she was claiming him as her own. And not only was she doing it, but her daughter was doing it, as well. Okay, so it had been eminently obvious last night that Skye knew something was happening between her and Brody. Still, to jump to the conclusion that she wanted to marry him...

Marry Brody? Why, she was barely getting used to the idea that the two of them were *getting involved*—strongly against her better judgment.

She should have known something like this would happen. Okay, so maybe there was no wife hidden away, or any kids. Just some time in the clink for pulverizing someone that he'd conveniently forgotten to mention.

Even as pain overwhelmed her, Kate told herself that, for it all, she should be grateful to Agnes. After all, she had begun to get quite carried away over Brody Baker, a man whom, in truth, she hardly knew. As Agnes Pilcher had so adeptly demonstrated.

I should have known better. I should have known better. The words spun like a litany in her head. She thought back to that first day when Brody Baker had literally come roaring into her life. That bike, the black leather jacket, those wild blond locks, that jaunty walk, the cocky expression. She'd thought he was one of those Hell's Angels. Two nights ago at his place, on the other hand, he'd been an angel straight from heaven—bringing her right up there with him.

Well, nothing like getting back down to earth. Only did she have to land quite so hard? Did it have to be this painful? Kate swallowed against the huge knot in her throat.

She looked up to see her ex-mother-in-law about to make her exit. She called out to her. Agnes half turned. "Yes, Kate?"

"You didn't . . . tell Skye, did you? About Brody? About his having been . . . in prison?"

"Really, Kate, what do you take me for? I do not feel that is suitable information for young ears." Agnes gave her a sharp look. "And I'd think if you were so concerned about Skye, you'd be more careful in future regarding—what shall we say?—your personal involvements with the opposite sex."

After Agnes's departure Kate was so preoccupied with her misery and guilt that she never even heard the knock on her door.

The instant Julie entered, she knew something was terribly wrong. Her sister had anguish written all over her face.

"What is it, Kate? What happened? You look like you just lost your best friend."

Kate stared misty-eyed across at her sister. "Best friend" wasn't the half of it.

Julie gestured over her shoulder with a wave of her thumb. "Don't tell me. This must have had something to do with Agnes Pilcher's visit. I saw her leaving just as I stepped out of my office. I tell you, Kate, I never fail to marvel that Agnes and Mellie Pilcher are actually sisters. Granted, Mellie's a little ditzy, but she's so sweet and kind. And you've got to admit she's adorable, with that halo of snowy white hair and those twinkling brown eyes and a smile that lights up a room. No trouble understanding why Dad adores her. But Agnes. She always looks—and acts—like she's just bitten into a particularly sour lemon. Can you imagine Dad ever having had a crush on her? Okay, that was back some forty years ago. But still. Thank God he married Mom. And we should count our blessings that if he had to go and fall for someone at this stage in his life that it was Mellie and not Agnes. I think that's one of the reasons Agnes has it in for the whole Hart family. She's bursting with jealousy. I bet she's still carrying the torch for Dad." Julie stopped abruptly and smiled as she eyed her sister. "How about if I shut up and you take a turn."

Kate sighed. "What's wrong with me, Julie?"

That was precisely what Julie had asked Kate a minute ago. "There's nothing wrong with you," Julie said firmly. "And if Agnes Pilcher said there was, well, Agnes Pilcher is sure that there's something wrong with everyone. Except her. Why are you letting her get to you all of a sudden?"

Kate wasn't really listening. "Oh, I know there must be some decent men out there."

Julie was confused. "How did we get from Agnes to the subject of men?"

Kate remained on her own track. "Ben's decent. So's Delaney. And Dad, of course. It must be me. There's got to be something wrong with me that I always fall for liars, cheats, con men, brawling ex-convicts. . . ."

"Hold on. The liars, cheats and con men, I think I can identify. But brawling ex-convicts? Now you've stumped me."

Kate shut her eyes to stem the tears that were starting to spill over her lids. "Brody," she croaked.

"Brody?"

"Brody."

"Wait. Are you telling me Brody Baker's an ex-con?"

"Yes."

"No."

"Yes," Kate said emphatically.

Julie sat down on the closest chair, feeling suddenly weak-kneed. "I don't believe it."

"Agnes wouldn't make it up. It's too easy to check," Kate said in a flat voice. "She's right. I should have checked more carefully before I hired him. It's all my fault."

"Wait a second. Exactly what did he do?" Julie demanded.

"He spent a year in jail for assault," Kate said, her expression desolate.

"Who did he assault? Why did he do it? When was it? Where was it? How did . . . ?"

"Stop. Stop playing the journalist, Julie," Kate pleaded, dropping her head in her hands. "I don't know the answers. I don't care what they are. I made a horrible mistake. . . ."

"That's not true," Julie challenged. "Brody Baker happens to be a terrific program director and you did not make a mistake hiring him."

Kate lifted her head and gave her sister a wan look. "That's not the mistake *I'm* talking about."

Julie raised an eyebrow. "Oh."

"Oh?" Kate echoed miserably. "Oh? Is that all you can say?"

"Come on, Kate. So, you're human. Let's face it. Brody Baker is pretty damn irresistible. And he's nuts about you. It was bound to happen. And knowing you, it wouldn't have unless you really did have very strong feelings for him."

"I have very strong feelings, all right. I hate him. He swore he was different, but he's just the same as all the rest. And I'm the same idiot I've always been when it comes to men."

"Why don't you talk to him, Kate? I'm sure he had his reasons. I'm sure he can explain. . . ."

"Oh, so am I," Kate said harshly. "They can always explain. It's amazing how good they are at explanations. Almost as good as they are at lying, cheating, deceiving—" The words caught in her throat and she couldn't go on.

"Well, if you won't talk to him, I will," Julie said firmly.

"No," Kate countered emphatically as Julie rose. "I'll talk to him. It'll be a very short talk. Two words. *You're fired.*"

KATE FOUND BRODY in the studio, finishing up some last-minute details with Gus about the first airing that day of the new "Mr. Fix-It" show. The set looked like a handyman's paradise, and Brody was in high spirits. After Gus took off, Brody crossed the studio to her with that loose, sexy stride of his, legs slightly bowed, arms swinging.

"Hi, I was just about to come looking for you," he said warmly.

Before Kate could respond, he swept her right into his arms. She let out a gasp of protest, but it was swallowed by Brody's mouth, which he pressed over hers with lightning speed and riveting passion.

For a moment, Kate's mind went catapulting back to their night in each other's arms, Brody's kiss distracting her with memories and sensations that she now bitterly regretted.

She shoved him away. "Please don't, Brody," she said stiffly.

He grinned. "Sorry, boss. I guess I got carried away. I've been waiting all morning to see you. I didn't sleep a wink again last night. Not that I'm complaining. I spent the whole night thinking about you. About what I'd have liked to be doing with you in that big, empty old bed of mine. Just thinking about it makes me hot all over, Katie. And look at you. You're all flushed yourself. Are you thinking what I'm thinking?"

"I seriously doubt it," Kate said archly.

Brody ruffled her hair. "Okay, boss lady. I'll behave on the job," he said, raising his right hand. "I promise."

Kate bit the insides of her cheeks. Promises. Oh, how easily men made them. Only to break them with impunity whenever it suited their needs or interests.

"How about we get away for lunch?" Brody was saying seductively. "I have an idea. We can go over to your house. Skye's in school so it'll be nice and quiet. We can pick up some sandwiches, eat them real fast and climb into your big bed. . . ."

"Brody. . ."

"And I've got dinner all planned. I thought we could take Skye out for Chinese, then drop her off at practice, then . . ."

The instant Kate heard Skye's name, a rush of anger and despair swept over her.

"Leave Skye out of this!" she shouted at him. "She's already going to be hurt enough as it is. That's what your deceptions have got you, Brody. A teenage girl with a broken heart. She's the one who's going to suffer."

Brody looked at Kate as if she'd gone nuts. "What are you talking about?"

"Forget about my heart. I can take some more hard knocks. I'm used to them. But Skye." She swallowed hard, fighting back tears. "I promised myself that after Arnie and I split I'd never subject her to that kind of hurt again. And then you came along, sprinkling stardust, looking like you just stepped off the cover of a romance novel, making her laugh, cooking her her favorite food, winning her heart, making her believe you'd won mine. She thinks you're the next best thing to Christmas."

Brody dug his hands into his jeans pockets as he regarded Kate with a mix of confusion and caution. "And what do you think?"

Kate's face turned hard. "I think you're a bastard."

Brody's face showed no expression at her attack. His voice remained low and even. "That's quite a change from what you were thinking only last night. I thought we'd reached some kind of understanding last night. I thought we were finally on the same wavelength. What happened, Kate? Did you have a bad dream or something?"

"I had a bad dream, all right. A real full-fledged nightmare. And I only wish it had happened while I was sleeping."

Brody's patience was beginning to wear thin. "Want to tell me what I'm being charged with?"

She laughed derisively. "Interesting way of putting it. Is that what you asked the cop when he arrested you? Is that what you asked the judge when you went to court?"

He glared at her. "What the hell are you talking about, Kate?"

She glared back. "Stop pretending, Brody. I know all about it. Your year in San Padres County Jail. For assault."

Brody didn't speak right away. He merely gave Kate a long, assessing look. "I see."

"I thought you would," she responded acidly.

"So you know all about it."

Kate compressed her lips. "I know everything I need to know. I want you out, Brody. You're . . . fired."

She started to turn, but he was too fast for her. He had a firm grip on her arm before she managed to do an about-face.

"Even the judge gave me a chance to have my say, Kate."

"This isn't a court of law," she said icily, even though she was burning up inside with pain and heartbreak.

"No, it isn't. How foolish of me not to see the difference. You don't play by any rules."

She glared at him. "I don't play by any rules? Why, of all the—"

"You've got me charged, convicted and sentenced without so much as knowing a single fact."

"You assaulted someone. You spent a year in jail. And you conveniently never brought it up, never indicated it on your résumé. Was that the real reason you were fired from your last job? Did you try to *distract* your last female boss, too, so she wouldn't do a background check? Only to have failed? Well, you failed here, too, buster. A little late, I grant you. Still, better late than never." She struggled to free herself from Brody's hold, but he refused to let her go. Rage boiled up in her.

"Why don't you just sock me, Brody? You're obviously not averse to resorting to violence."

Brody narrowed his eyes and leaned closer to her. They were practically nose-to-nose. "Believe me, Kate, you're tempting me. Right this minute, I'm itching to throw you over my knee and spank you. It's only that you're Skye's mom that I'm holding back. I know it would upset her. And I wouldn't want to upset that girl for the world. Like I told you last night, I happen to think your daughter's terrific. It's her mom I'm starting to have my doubts about."

"Well, I feel the same way about you," Kate retorted.

"Oh, no. You're way ahead of me, Kate. You've been tormented by doubts right from the moment you set eyes on me. You were so sure I'd hurt you that the minute you thought you had anything on me, you seized on it like it was your lifeline."

He released his grip on her arm like it had suddenly burned him. "You're right. This isn't a court. You don't have to ask me for any explanations. And I don't have to give you any. You want me out? I'm out. I'll go pack up my stuff and be cleared out in an hour."

"Fine."

Only he made no move. It was like he was rooted to the spot. And she was, too. There was nothing holding her there. All she had to do was make her exit. Leave Brody to pack up his gear and get out. Out of the station. Out of her life.

So, why couldn't she leave? Because she realized, standing there, that whatever her feelings were about what Brody had done in the past, nothing could be worse than the agonizing sense of loss she felt at that moment. She was in love with him. That was the cold, hard truth. Fight against it though she might, it had happened.

Brody's voice cut through the awful silence. "I know how these things spread like wildfire around town, so I think I'll set the record straight—for Skye if not for you. It wasn't a year, Kate. It was ninety days. I turned twenty in jail. Not a fun way to spend your birthday," he said in a flat voice.

"I got into an argument with a guy in a movie theater. I was with my girl and he was sitting on the other side of her. He made a pass at her. She got all upset. I asked him to step outside with me. He grinned, then made a grab at my date. She started to cry. And that's when I hit him. Square in the jaw. After which, I snatched my girl and walked on out of the theater."

He let out a long sigh. "It turned out this joker was the local police chief's son. I'd socked the chief's precious boy in the jaw and the chief saw to it that the judge socked me with a verdict of guilty. I had a choice. Pay a fine or take the ninety days. I was young. Idealistic, I guess. I felt that paying up when I wasn't the one in the wrong was adding insult to injury. So I sat it out in jail for three months, feeling like a martyr. You know what the worst of it was?"

Kate couldn't look Brody in the eye. She felt small and ashamed. In a way, she had been no better than the police chief or the judge. Worse than either, really. "No, but . . . I can imagine," she whispered, her throat having gone dry.

"She dumped me."

Kate's eyes shot up to Brody's face. "She didn't?"

"Worse still, she started dating the police chief's son. Go figure women out. I sure can't begin to do it." Only he wasn't talking about women in general at that moment or the girl who'd jilted him for the police chief's son. Kate knew he was talking specifically about her.

"Oh, Brody," she murmured, her voice filled with sympathy.

"I forgot all about it. The girl and the stint in jail. That's why I didn't put it down on my résumé. It was more than seventeen years ago. I was just a kid. Anyway, I never really saw it as a crime I'd committed."

Kate struggled to find some way to apologize, but she didn't know how.

"If it's okay with you, I'll clean out my office later. Right now, I need to just—" But Brody couldn't finish the sentence, couldn't tell her what he needed. Instead, he brushed past her and strode quickly down the hall, out the main door.

10

For a few moments Kate couldn't believe he'd actually left. Then, in a panic, she raced down the hall after him.

She was breathless by the time she got to the parking lot at the side of the building where Brody, who must have sprinted once he hit the outside, was gunning his Harley.

"Brody."

His eyes fixed on her. He rode his bike right up to where she was standing.

The sun was surprisingly warm, the day mellow for early November. And yet Kate felt a shiver run through her. "Brody, I'm . . . sorry."

He gave her a searching look. "So am I, Katie," he murmured, then revved the bike's engine and rode past her.

He's leaving. He's going to race that Harley right out of this parking lot, down Main Street, and just keep right on going. And he's not even going to look back. Oh, Kate, you've gone and done it. You've blown it big time. Oh, you can blame it on Agnes, but Brody was right: You were looking for something to pin your fears and doubts on.

Suddenly the bike squealed to a stop just at the edge of the lot.

"Get on," Brody barked.

He wasn't even looking at her. She wasn't even sure he was talking to her. It didn't matter. She ran the distance separating them and hopped on behind him, wrapping her arms around his waist.

They sped through town, their hair blowing every which way, stinging their cheeks. Even though it was relatively warm for November, the wind cut through them and Kate pressed more tightly against Brody's back. It was so good to be holding on to him. She shut her eyes and felt all the strain and anger of the morning rush out of her like some awful fever.

Brody drove up a winding mountain road, then down a dirt path to a natural spring in a grassy clearing on the outskirts of Pittsville.

Kate looked around in surprise. "This is my favorite spot. How did you...?" She finished the sentence with a little laugh. "Skye?"

"Your favorite flower, your favorite poet, your favorite getaway spot. I also know your favorite color," he said, gently cupping her hands, which were still wrapped around his waist. "It's blue."

"Yes. Like your eyes," she whispered

He helped her off the bike and turned her to him, his hands gripping her arms. After a moment or two he loosened his hold and slid his hands down to her wrists, drawing them behind her back so that she arched naturally into him.

He smiled tenderly, the sunlight making his wild hair glisten like spun gold. He was the stuff of dreams, all right.

"Brody, about all the things I said to you back in your studio..."

He stilled her by pressing his lips to hers, kissing her lightly. "I should have been straight with you. Now you know everything. There are no more secrets."

"You were just a kid. And I'm glad you socked him. And that you stood by your principles."

He nuzzled her neck. "So, you're not sore at me anymore?"

"I should have given you a chance to explain. I was scared. I'm still scared. This is all happening so fast...."

"Don't be scared, Katie. You are the best thing that has ever happened to me."

Kate felt overwhelmed by Brody's words, by his fresh, woodsy smell, by the heat of his body pressed against hers.

"Brody." She tried to say more, but her throat seemed to shut down; her need for him was so piercing, she thought she would burst with it.

He released her wrists and cupped her face in his hands. "I love you, Kate. And I want you to trust me. I'm not going to break your heart. I'm not going to break Skye's heart. Or disappoint her. Just stop fighting so hard, Katie. Give me a chance."

Kate averted her gaze. "It's all happening so fast. I need time, Brody."

"We'll take it real slow if that's the way you want it."

He started to release her, but she threw her arms around him, holding him fast. "Not that slow," she said with a wanton smile.

He scrutinized her, his mouth curving into a teasing smile. "You mean you want me?"

"I want you."

"Right here? Right now? Wasn't that you who was telling me you're very reserved?"

She shook her head, twining her arms around his neck, her lips finding their way to his neck. "That must have been someone else."

"This is pretty wild and daring, Katie."

"You *make* me feel wild and daring, Brody Baker."

"This is my fault, is it?"

"Oh, yes. Yes, it's all your fault," she said, pulling back to brazenly tug her turtleneck sweater over her head.

"You'll be cold," he warned playfully, even though it did happen, as if by magic, to be one of the warmest November days on record for the region. Even the fates were with them.

She grinned, her eyes sparkling. "You wanna bet?"

They both began undressing in a rush. Brody's biggest struggle was getting his boots off. Kate knelt down to help him with the second boot, tumbling backward as the boot came off. She gave a little shriek as her naked body made contact with the cool, wet grass, but then she lifted her head skyward and gazed up at the puffs of snowy cloud drifting across the blue sky. She laughed softly at nothing in particular except that she felt so deliciously happy.

After divesting himself of his jeans and briefs in one quick move, Brody bent down, caught hold of Kate and lifted her up into his arms. She spied both desire and amusement lurking in his eyes.

"You ever do it on a bike, babe?" he drawled, climbing with her still in his arms onto the leather double seat of his Harley. They were facing each other; Kate was on Brody's lap.

She smiled sheepishly. "Only in my dreams, Brody. Only in my dreams."

"Well, Katie, I'm going to make your dreams come true," he murmured, pulling her closer.

Kate felt a flash of concern, knowing that it was possible someone might come by. The vision of public shame was momentarily disquieting, but then Brody was lifting her slightly off him, making certain adjustments. No sooner was he inside her than she instantly lost touch with propriety—with everything, for that matter, but the sweet rush of sensation as he filled her.

They moved in tune with each other, as Brody's mouth found its way to her breast, drawing a taut nipple deep inside. Even the rhythm of their breathing blended together in perfect harmony for a time. Then Kate's breathing went haywire, coming in fast little spurts as she felt herself being carried over the edge.

Brody thrust deeper and deeper, with his feet planted on the ground on either side of the bike to keep it from tipping. Her head flung back, Kate rode him at an ever-more-frantic pace until she began to dissolve into rapturous ecstasy, an ecstasy that had always eluded her—until Brody. Within moments, she felt him explode, too, and she relished his joy as much as her own.

Afterward, while they lay embracing on the cool grass, once again fully dressed, Kate felt a powerful sense of connection, not only with Brody, but with all of her surroundings—the blue sky, the puffy white clouds, the brilliant sun, the swaying pines, the bubbling stream. She now saw that this little oasis in the mountains, which she had long ago chosen as her special space, had always been lacking something. Until now. Until Brody Baker.

Her sigh was rich in contentment as she felt the gentle press of his lips on her temple. The feeling, however, was short-lived.

"We could get married in the spring, Katie. The spring is months away. Plenty of time for us to get better acquainted," Brody added with a warm laugh.

No sooner had he spoken than the sun slipped behind a cloud, the sky suddenly turned gray and it felt to Kate as if all the vivid color had abruptly vanished from the landscape.

She sat up, feeling as if all the color and life had drained from her, as well. "Brody, I can't marry you. Not in the spring. Not . . . ever."

"Come on, Kate. You can't mean . . ."

"There's something I've got to tell you. . . ."

KATE WAS PARKED in her car outside the high school at three that afternoon. Kids started pouring out the doors and after a few minutes she spotted her daughter making her exit, chattering away with her best friend, Alice, and Robby Mitchell, the boy Kate suspected Skye had a crush on. She gave a little sigh. Oh, to be young again and for life not to be fraught with complications. And then she saw Alice and Robby break away from Skye and head in the opposite direction. Hand in hand. For the briefest moment Kate spied the stricken expression on Skye's face, only to be quickly replaced with a big smile as another boy who was passing by stopped to say a couple of words to her.

Kate felt her chest constrict at the anguish and disappointment she knew her daughter had to be feeling. Maybe life was never simple, no matter how old—or young—you were.

Skye continued alone down the school's concrete path and Kate gave a little toot of her horn to get her attention. Skye looked around and when she spotted her mom, seemed clearly surprised to see her. Understandable since Kate rarely picked her daughter up at school; her workday usually went on till at least five o'clock, often later.

Skye hurried over, her backpack thumping against her. She quickly opened the passenger-side door, bent forward and peered in. "Anything wrong? Nobody died or anything?" she asked anxiously.

Kate forced a smile. "No, kiddo. Nobody died or anything. I just thought we could spend a little time together. Unless you've already made plans."

Skye's gaze shifted momentarily down the street in the direction that Alice and Robby had headed. "No," she said with a shrug. "No plans."

"Well, then, hop in."

Skye hesitated for a moment. "It's not something I did wrong, is it?"

"No. You didn't do anything wrong. Let's take a drive out to Monroe."

"Monroe? That's, like, close to a two-hour drive. Why are we driving to Monroe?"

"Are you worried about the time because you've got a lot of homework?" Kate asked, as Skye slipped off her knapsack, flung it in the back and slid into the passenger seat.

"No. Hardly any. I had two free periods today, so I got most of it done. I've just got to study for a vocab test."

"I can go over the definitions with you at dinner," Kate suggested, as they pulled out. "We can eat at that cute little Italian place in Monroe. Mia Cucina. You loved it the last time we ate there a few months ago."

"Sounds great," Skye said, her words more optimistic than her tone.

When Kate got to the first intersection she turned left onto Route 32, heading east. Skye glanced over at her mother. "What's that in your hair?"

Kate's hand darted up to her head. "In my hair?" She pulled out a blade of grass, quickly scrunching it up in her palm. "Nothing. Something the wind must have blown in."

"Do you know you're speeding? We just passed a thirty-five-miles-an-hour sign," Skye warned. "Are we in some kind of a hurry for some reason?"

"No. No, we've got all the time in the world." Kate slowed down and glanced over at her daughter. "Wasn't that Alice and Robby I saw you with coming out of school?"

Skye hesitated. "Yeah. They're both in my last-period class. Earth sciences. Yuck."

"I was never crazy about science myself." Except for her very recent advanced class in the birds and the bees . . .

"He's such a jerk," Skye muttered.

"Robby?"

"No," Skye said with a look of surprise. "Mr. Mason. My science teacher. Why would I think Robby was a jerk?"

"I don't know. I guess I just thought . . . Well, boys that age often are. Jerks, that is."

"Well, Robby isn't a jerk. He's . . . great."

"Oh."

"Next to Alice, he's my best friend. My best boy friend. As in friend who's a boy," she made a point of clarifying.

"And is he . . . Alice's best boy friend, too?" Kate asked gently.

Skye stared out the window. "Robby's had a crush on Alice for ages."

"And Alice? Has she had a crush on Robby all that time?"

"Yeah, but she wouldn't admit it."

"Why was that?"

"Remember when she went away to camp last summer?"

Kate nodded.

"Well, she fell head over heels for some guy who really was a jerk. And I guess, after he dumped her, she ended up feeling the way you do. That all guys are jerks. Robby included."

"That's not how I feel," Kate said softly. "I guess sometimes I'm quick to mouth off, but I don't want you to think that I think . . ."

Skye grinned. "Yeah, I know you don't think Brody's a jerk. You . . . couldn't."

Kate looked over and saw that her daughter's cheeks were a bright red. She felt her own cheeks heat up in response.

"You're right. I don't think Brody's a jerk, Skye."

Skye looked expectantly over at her mother. "Neither do I."

"I guessed that."

"And he thinks you're terrific. He told me so."

Kate smiled wistfully, and was silent for a couple of minutes. Then she said offhandedly, "Your grandma stopped by my office today."

Skye gave her mother an uneasy glance. "She...did?"

"Yes, she did."

Skye picked at a loose thread on her jacket cuff. "I guess I forgot to mention it."

"I guess you did."

"The thing is, I hadn't seen her for a while and I thought it would be nice—"

"Who told you about the alimony arrangement I have with your dad?"

Skye frowned. "You *are* mad at me. I knew it. That's why you picked me up at school."

"No, Skye," Kate tried to assure her. "I'm not mad at you. Honest. I do wish you'd discussed the matter with me first, but—"

"I was only trying to help, Mom."

"I know you were."

"I thought it wasn't fair that you'd have to make a choice between the station and getting married again."

"Who told you I wanted to get married?"

"Come on, Mom. You just have to look at you and Brody together. It's written over both your faces. Ask anyone if you don't believe me. Aunt Julie. Aunt Rachel. Even Grandpa Leo and Mellie . . ."

"Oh, Skye," Kate said, her voice thick with frustration.

"Just like we all know how important WPIT is to you. To all of us. And so I thought maybe there was some way you wouldn't need to make a choice. . . ."

Kate rested a hand lightly on her daughter's shoulders. "Skye, I made my choice a long time ago. That's why I agreed to the arrangement with your father. I tried marriage once. It wasn't for me."

"It was all Dad's fault," Skye argued.

"No, Skye," Kate said emphatically. "It wasn't all your dad's fault. Sure, what he did was wrong. Very wrong. But we were having our problems long before Sue Ellen ever came to Pittsville. We both contributed to those problems."

"Okay, but still, it doesn't mean that you'd have the same problems with Brody," Skye persisted. "Dad and Brody are so different, Mom. I never remember Dad bringing you even one bouquet of tulips."

"What I'm trying to say, Skye, is that I think we've managed quite nicely all these years, just the two of us. I don't want to mess up a good thing."

"Sure, we have done fine without a man, but in a way that's the point. It's not always going to be the two of us, Mom," Skye lectured in a voice that strikingly resembled her mother's. Kate had to smile at how the roles had gotten switched.

"Face it, Mom," Skye went on. "I'll be off to college in next to no time. And then it won't be the two of us any more. It'll be just you. All alone in that big house. No one there when you get home from work. Cooking for one every night. No one to talk to, or..."

"You make it sound like you're leaving next month," Kate said with a gentle smile. "Four years isn't exactly next to no time, Skye." She felt a need to change the subject. You still want to go to Columbia like Aunt Julie and major in journalism, right?"

"Yeah, sure I do, but..."

"But what?"

"A college like Columbia costs a lot of money."

"Hey, WPIT is moving very nicely into the black and I'm hoping that in four years we'll be sitting pretty."

"You'll be sitting alone."

"Skye."

"But what about Brody, Mom? You love him, don't you? And he loves you."

"We care for each other, Skye. When you're as old as I am, you don't toss words like *love* around cavalierly. I'm not saying that Brody isn't a terrific guy. Terrific enough to understand that I have responsibilities, obligations . . ."

"Oh, Mom, now you sound like a martyr."

"Really, Skye, where do you come up with such notions?"

"Aunt Julie and Aunt Rachel think so, too."

"What is this? Are the three of you in cahoots, here?"

"They say it's just that you're scared."

The timbre of Kate's voice shifted. "And what do they say I'm scared of?"

Skye sighed. "The institution of marriage."

Kate laughed. "The institution, huh?"

"It's no laughing matter, Mom," Skye said, hurt creeping into her voice. After all, she was trying to have a very adult conversation with her mother.

"I'm sorry," Kate apologized immediately, reading her daughter's mind.

"Aunt Julie says that you think marriage was created by divorce lawyers."

Kate thought that "Aunt Julie" had been saying a little too much to her fourteen-year-old niece. She made a mental note to have a word or two with her sister.

"I bet Aunt Julie and Ben never get divorced. Or Aunt Rachel and Delaney. Marriage can last forever, Mom. I bet you and Brody—"

"I am not going to marry Brody, Skye. And it's got nothing to do with being a martyr or being afraid of the institution of marriage."

"It's the station, then. Which is why I wanted Grandma Agnes to try to get Dad—"

"We have a contract, honey. A contract we both agreed to."

"So let him have the dumb old station if that's the way he wants to be," Skye said, sounding very much like a little girl again.

Kate sighed. "I wish it were easy to explain to you—" She stopped. It *wasn't* easy to explain to her daughter. Any more than it had been easy to explain to Brody—even though she'd tried. To give him his due, he had tried to understand, but there were feelings she hadn't been able to put adequately into words.

WPIT wasn't merely her livelihood. Or merely the livelihood of practically her whole family. It was a way of life for all of them. Losing the station would mean losing more than a business; it would mean letting everyone down, losing her roots, losing her sense of security and well-being.

If she didn't have the station, she'd very likely have to move someplace else in order to find a decent job. And uproot Skye. They'd have to leave everyone they knew and loved; leave a place where they'd always felt safe and content. Not to mention what would become of her sisters, Ben, Meg, Gus, all the rest of the gang at WPIT. Agnes might keep some of them on, but not any of the Hart family. Not that any of her family would want to stay. Julie, Rachel, Ben—they'd all be out of a job. They might all have to move away from Pittsville, a town that had become home to all of them. And it would be her fault.

Then there was Brody. At first, when she'd told him about losing the station if they got married, he'd shrugged it off. "So we'll pack up and find us another station," he'd said.

It was simple enough for Brody to pack up and move on. He didn't have the attachments, the ties, the responsibilities. He didn't have a family here, lifetime friends. And there was no way to make him fully understand how much the station had come to mean to her. Running WPIT formed an essential part of her identity. It gave her a sense of self-esteem and accomplishment, both of which had been sorely missing in her life, especially during her nine-year marriage to Arnie. A marriage that had ended in failure. A failure she'd vowed a long time ago never to repeat.

For all that, it hadn't been easy turning down Brody's marriage proposal. She did love him. Maybe even enough to take another chance at marriage. But there was simply too much at stake and too much to lose all around. And then, what if it didn't work out? Could she go through the heartbreak of another divorce? Put Skye through it? She could see how attached Skye had already become to Brody.

"Mom?" Skye's voice shook Kate from her thoughts.

She sighed. "It's awfully complicated, Skye. You're just going to have to trust that I'm making the right decision for all of us."

"Why couldn't you buy the station from Dad?" Skye asked stubbornly. "We could ask him what he'd want for it."

"Even if he would sell it, which I don't think he would, whatever the price, I couldn't pay it."

"I really don't have to go to some place like Columbia, Mom," Skye said, knowing her mother was already putting money away each week into a special college fund for her. "I could go to a state university. It would cost way less. . . ."

Kate squeezed her daughter's knee. "Enough talk about all that. Let's talk about something else, okay?"

Skye folded her arms over her chest. "What does Brody think about all this?"

Kate shot her daughter a glance. "That isn't exactly something else."

"Well, I bet he's not going to take this lying down. Not Brody," Skye said emphatically.

Kate gripped the wheel more tightly. "So, when's your next basketball game?"

"Tuesday," Skye said. And after the briefest of pauses, she added, "Brody's coming."

11

WHILE KATE AND SKYE were over in Monroe that evening having a strained dinner at Mia Cucina, Brody sat alone at the counter at the Full Moon Café, morosely working on his fourth refill of black coffee.

"How 'bout something to fill your belly?" Betty asked, as she topped off his mug. "We've got pot roast on special. It's delicious."

"No, thanks," Brody muttered, stirring some sugar into his coffee. "I'm not hungry."

Betty reached across the counter and patted his arm. "My oldest boy, Mikey, got into a little tiff with the law himself a few years back. Had a bit too much to drink at a party and then some thugs from Louden decided to crash the party and Mikey took on a few of them. There was a number of black eyes—two on Mikey—and a lot of broken furniture. He got off with a big lecture from the judge and an even bigger one from me, and a year's probation. Now he's married and the father of two. And he's never been in trouble since."

Brody smiled. "Neither have I."

"I knew it," Betty said, giving him a hearty tap on the shoulder. "You never did impress me as a troublemaker."

Brody gave her a brief rundown of the *true* story, hoping to nip in the bud the rumors that were obviously spreading through town.

Betty chuckled. "Well, by the time I heard about it, I've got to tell you, Brody, it was a lot more exciting than the real version. Not that I bought it, mind you. I've lived in this town too long to believe even half of what I hear. And the half I do believe, I only believe half of, if you catch my drift."

Brody nodded, then took a sip of coffee. "Anyway, that's not my problem at the moment," Brody said despondently. "I told Kate the way it really was and she saw it wasn't nearly as bad as her ex-mother-in-law made it out to be."

"That Agnes," Betty said, rolling her eyes. "What can I say? Deep down, I think she's just plain unhappy so she figures why should anyone else be happy. Unfortunately, especially Kate."

"Because of the divorce?" Brody asked.

Betty slid a piece of blueberry pie onto a plate and set it down beside Brody's mug. "Arnie was all Agnes had. In her eyes, that boy could do no wrong. You see, her husband died when Arnie was a baby and it was just the two of them. Agnes never remarried, although I know she would have liked to."

"Oh?"

Betty leaned over the counter and lowered her voice, even though the café was empty save for some locals in two end booths out of earshot. "Agnes Pilcher has had a thing for Kate's dad for ages. They even courted for a brief time in their youth. Really must eat away at her that of *all* people, her own sister, Mellie, got him in the end. Which is another thing she's got against the Harts."

"None of which is any of their faults," Brody said, stabbing a piece of pie with his fork. He wasn't hungry but it gave him something to do.

"Who says life's fair?" Betty said with a wistful smile, turning at the ding of the pickup bell to grab a couple of the pot-roast specials and bring them to a couple sitting at the end booth.

When she came back she once again topped off Brody's coffee mug. "Look, if you want to talk about it..." she coaxed.

It didn't take much coaxing. "I asked Kate to marry me."

Betty's eyes lit up. "You did? Already?" She tapped her index finger against her lip. "Now let me think. Who's the winner?"

"The winner?" Brody asked, bewildered. All he knew was the loser. Himself.

"We started a pool," Betty confided. "Must be at least two-dozen folk got in on it. Gus. I do believe it was Gus. I'm almost sure he picked three weeks. Or less than a month, anyway. I said you'd pop the question on Christmas Eve. I thought, you being the romantic type and all—"

"She said no," Brody interrupted. "Anyone bet on her answer?"

"You mean she turned you down cold?"

"I sure felt cold all over."

"Oh, she'll change her mind. You wait and see."

"Not if her ex-husband or his mother have any say in the matter. And apparently they have quite a lot to say," Brody added sardonically.

Betty clasped her hands together. "Why, I forgot all about that. You're right. The station does revert back to Arnie Pilcher if Kate remarries. Oh, dear. Giving up WPIT. It's been Kate's for so many years now, I guess a lot of us kind of forgot that she stood to lose it if she got hitched again."

The waitress shook her head. "Doesn't seem fair. She's put her heart and soul into that station. Why, it was nothing much when Arnie and Agnes were running the show. A couple of local news pieces and then old, boring reruns. No, it just doesn't seem fair she'd have to hand it back to the Pilchers now that it's getting to be so successful."

"Who said life's fair?" Brody countered with a grim smile.

"I know. I know."

"It would be one thing if I'd lost out to another guy," Brody said forlornly. "But to lose out to a television station."

"I was one of many who advised Kate not to agree to the arrangement," Betty said. "Several of us saw it as a bad idea. Especially her dad. Leo's a real romantic, himself. Look at him and Mellie. You do know they're planning on getting hitched in June. You never know when it can happen again to a person, no matter how old you get. Which was why me and Leo and several others did our best to talk Kate out of agreeing to give the station back to Arnie, just in case Mr. Right ever did come along and she wanted to remarry."

"Maybe if she believed the guy really was Mr. Right, holding on to the station wouldn't come first."

"Oh, she knows you're Mr. Right, all right," Betty said emphatically. "We all do. Still, you gotta understand what WPIT means to Kate."

Brody sighed. "I'm beginning to understand more and more. It's just so damn . . . frustrating."

"I still say if she'd held out," Betty said, "I bet anything her lawyer could have worked out a better deal. Split the station down the middle so she could have bought out his half. Agnes might have balked—everyone knows she wants to run that station, which Arnie would gladly let her do. I'll bet you anything Arnie's new wife would have persuaded him to take the money and run. That Sue Ellen sure likes living high off the hog."

Betty sighed. "But Kate dug in her heels and swore up and down that there was no way in hell—pardon my French—that she was ever going to do something as dumb as get married again, so the deal was fine with her. That girl is just about the most stubborn Hart around. And they're all a pretty stubborn bunch."

Brody poked his chest. "Well, I come from a long line of stubborn Bakers. And I'm the stubbornest of the lot."

Betty grinned. "That's the ticket. I knew you wouldn't give up easy."

"Like my daddy used to say," Brody drawled, "nothin' worth having ever came easy. If you want something bad enough . . ."

November 9

Mom can swear up and down till Doomsday that she just "cares" for Brody, but I know the truth. She does love him. A thousand times more than she ever loved that jerk, Oscar. Brody's the real thing.

All the kids at school who have stepdads are always bad-mouthing them. But if Brody were my stepdad, I know I would never do that. Brody's different. Even though he's absolutely gaga over Mom, he always pays attention to me, wants to come to my practices and games, does something so sweet like making me my favorite food. He makes the absolutely best barbecued ribs I ever tasted. And he's so cool. Every girl in my school has a crush on him. Even Alice. Which I personally don't think is being fair to Robby.

And that's another thing. Brody's the only one in the whole world I've told about how I really feel about Robby. He understood. And he was so sweet. I blush every time I think about what he said to me. He told me that I was really special and that one of these days Robby or maybe some boy that was even more awesome than Robby was going to fall head over heels in love with me. Oh, not that I actually believe that's true, but it was just so nice of Brody to say that. And I keep thinking, if he was my stepdad, I know I could always go to him with stuff. Not that I don't go to my mom about a lot of things, but there are just some times you want a man's perspective.

The thing is, how's Brody ever going to get to be my stepdad if he and my mom don't get married, right? And it's as clear as the nose on my face, as Grandpa Leo says, that Mom's not ever going to even consider marrying Brody if it means giving the station back to Dad and Grandma Agnes.

Boy, going to see Grandma Agnes sure backfired. She was not the least ways receptive to my suggestion that she have a talk with Dad about the alimony arrangement. I tried to explain to her how important the station was to Mom and I raved about how great a job she was doing. Especially now that Brody was the program director—all the new shows he's starting and how he's revamping the scheduling, getting more syndicated shows, and working with Mom and Aunt Rachel on getting more national advertisers.

So there I am, raving on and on, and Grandma Agnes is sitting there in that big high-backed green velvet chair in the parlor looking at me like I was talking pure gibberish. And then it turns out that's exactly what she did think I was talking, because when I finally ran out of steam, she broke into this big lecture about how Mom was going to run the station right into the ground, even adding that a big reason was because of Brody, of all people. She kept dropping these hints like there was something wrong with Brody. She even said outright at one point that he was "no good." And as far as my dad wanting to let Mom keep the station if she and Brody got married, my grandmother treated that as some big joke.

The worst part, though, was her saying not to worry. In her opinion there was no likelihood at all that Mom would be marrying Brody even if my dad handed the station over to her wrapped in a big red ribbon. I was dying to ask her why she said that, but my grandmother told me it was time for her nap. God, she even suggested I go home and take a nap myself. She treats me like I never grew past five years old or something.

Not that Mom's treating me like I'm all that much older. Picking me up from school, driving clear out to Monroe for a dinner that she hardly even touched. And being so adamant about not loving Brody and not wanting to marry him, when she knows and I know it isn't in the least ways true.

Grown-ups! Really, there are days I think I'm more mature than the whole bunch of them.

SOON AFTER SKYE finished writing in her journal that evening, her gaze drifted over to her bedside phone. What harm would it do to give her dad a call? It had been a while since she'd spoken to him. Not that she'd ever ask him if he'd be willing to give the station to her mom for keeps even if she did get married again. Knowing her dad, he wouldn't take the question seriously. And even if he did, after her little chat with her grandmother, she realized it was a waste of time to imagine that was a possibility.

Okay, so he wouldn't give it to her Mom. That didn't mean that he might not *sell* it to her, even if her *mother* didn't think so. Skye could simply call and ask him how much it would cost to buy the station.

The more she thought about it, the better she liked the idea. Her dad was always complaining about how her stepmother spent money like it grew on trees. And Sue Ellen wasn't even working anymore. Plus, he had three new kids to raise and Sue Ellen had told her last time she'd visited that she wanted her kids to go to private school because all the children in the neighborhood who went to public schools were "unruly heathens." Private schooling for three kids had to cost a bundle, too. Not that her dad wasn't doing well at the investment firm where he was working. Grandma Agnes was always bragging about how successful he was. Then again, she would always add that a person could never have too much success. Or, in that case, Skye reasoned, too much money.

How her mom was going to come up with the money to buy the station was another matter altogether, but Skye decided, as she reached for the phone, that she'd tackle one problem at a time.

LEO HART, looking quite like a distinguished judge with his thick gray hair and finely chiseled features, rapped the gavel on the table. Well, actually, it wasn't a gavel. It was Mellie's wooden meat tenderizer, but it worked just fine to bring the noisy group to order.

The group consisted of Leo and Mellie, Julie and Ben, Rachel and Delaney, and Skye, who was the brainchild of this meeting of the Hart family.

"Please, let's have one person speak at a time," Leo said. "We all have ideas about how to go about financing the purchase of the station, but we're not going to get very far if everybody speaks up at once." He motioned to Julie, who was sitting to his right. "Why don't you start off?"

Julie nodded. "Before I offer my thoughts, I want to go on record as officially thanking Skye, here, for her initiative."

Skye beamed. Getting a compliment, especially from Aunt Julie whom she idolized, was a big deal.

Rachel seconded her sister. "Absolutely. We wouldn't be here trying to come up with a plan if Skye hadn't phoned her dad and actually wangled a figure out of him."

Leo ruffled his granddaughter's hair. "Watch out you don't get a swelled head, now," he said affectionately.

"Kudos to Skye, of course, but we have to all bear in mind that Arnie's asking price is...overinflated, to say the least," Ben said, hating to put a damper on the proceedings.

"I think if we can get within the ballpark amount," Leo said, "we may be able to talk him down some."

"I'm for the idea of selling stocks in the station. WPIT is a solid investment and a lot of people in and around Pittsville would jump at the chance to buy shares. I think it's a first-class solution," Julie said, shaking her head as Mellie came by with second servings of her apple-crumb cake.

"With Kate retaining controlling interest, naturally," Rachel piped in.

"How many shares would we be able to sell?" Ben asked. "At what price per share? I repeat, Arnie's asking price is pretty stiff."

"I'd like to give him a stiff upper lip," Delaney muttered. "You'd think he was selling the Taj Mahal, for what he's asking."

Rachel nudged her husband. Delaney looked apologetically over at Skye. Whatever they all might be feeling about Arnie Pilcher's greed, the man was Skye's father. "Sorry, sweetheart."

Skye shrugged. "Hey, at least he's willing to sell."

"I hate to put another fly in the ointment, here," Leo said, "but what's to stop Arnie from selling to someone else instead of Kate, once he gets the ownership back? We all know that Agnes has been itching to get her hands on the station again. She might just turn around and make her own deal with her son. After all, she'd like nothing better than to regain control of WPIT."

"We'll just get Dad to promise he'll only sell it to Mom," Skye said.

"The thing to do is for Kate to get the purchase-and-sale papers signed as soon as possible," Julie said. "I bet we could put up enough of a deposit to get things moving."

"Maybe," Delaney said. "But we'd have to guarantee that she could come up with the full amount for the purchase. Which brings us back to where we started."

"Well, we don't have to come up with all the money for the purchase," Ben said. "Just enough to back up a loan from the bank."

"I talked with Red Henderson over at First Trust," Leo said. All eyes turned expectantly to him. One look and they knew the news wasn't good. "He wasn't too encouraging," Leo confirmed. "It's not like WPIT is a big moneymaking proposition right at this time. Sure, it's growing, but the way Red put it, for the bank to finance a big portion of its purchase, they would have to see some pretty good figures. A lot better ones than I'm afraid we've got to show at the moment, from what you say, Rachel."

"It's not fair to judge the station at this point," Rachel countered. "Now that Brody's on board, I know we're going to see the profits rise substantially over the next couple of years."

"The thing is," Ben said, "is Brody likely to hang around here for two years? I confess if I'd believed Julie wasn't going to give in and marry me, I might have taken off myself, back when. It would have been too painful to stick around, seeing her every day, knowing she'd never be mine."

Julie slipped her hand into Ben's. "God, that's so romantic, honey."

Skye stared them all down. "Brody won't leave. He won't. He loves my mom too much to quit trying to get her to marry him. You'll see."

Everyone around the table smiled and nodded. While they didn't want to raise Skye's hopes, none of them had the heart to dash them, either. "How much does Red say we'd need to come up with?" Delaney asked his father-in-law.

"He says the bank may agree to a forty/sixty split. Meaning we'd have to come up with forty percent of the final negotiated price."

"We'd have to come up with almost half of the money?" Rachel asked incredulously. There was a hushed silence around the table. Forty percent was far more than any of them had imagined they'd have to come up with.

"I figure I could mortgage the house," Leo said. "Should bring in a nice penny since I own it free and clear."

"We don't have much built up in our place," Rachel said, "but we could apply for an equity note. It should bring us in a few thousand." She looked over at Ben, who nodded.

"We could do the same," Julie said. "Only it won't be very much since we were able to buy the house with such a small down payment and we've owned it for less than a year."

They all quoted figures and Skye did the totaling on her calculator. When she'd finished, she didn't look exactly elated. "That gives us about ten percent of what we need."

"I've got a little nest egg tucked away," Mellie said, setting a second serving of cake on Leo's plate.

"No, Mellie, we can't ask you..." Leo started to protest.

"Why not? I'm almost family, aren't I?" She wagged a finger at Leo. "You better not think even for one moment that I'm letting you off the hook, Leo Hart. We have a date at the church in June and you better be there."

He took her hand in his and squeezed. "With bells on," he murmured, giving her a hand a little peck.

Skye sighed. "I bet Brody really would wear bells."

"Okay," Julie said, determined to inject a note of optimism into the proceedings. "Let's start looking at our glass of water as half full instead of half empty."

"You mean ten-percent full," Rachel said morosely.

12

"WELL, THIS IS Mr. Fix-It saying good-night to all you fixer-uppers out there. Until next week. Remember, if there's something that needs fixing, there's always a way to fix it."

Gus, standing beside camera two, cued in the closing music, then gestured with a wave of his index finger in Harry Beckman's direction. "And that's a wrap."

Kate was standing on the sidelines, Harry Beckman's closing words echoing in her mind. If only it were true that there was a way to fix everything. Could Mr. Fix-It fix a broken heart?

She watched Brody, who was standing on the opposite side of the studio, walk over to Harry and give him a congratulatory pat on the back. She knew she should go over and congratulate Harry, as well. It really had been a good show. Even better than the first one last week. She felt confident they had another successful show on their hands, thanks as much to Brody, who'd created it, as to Harry Beckman, who'd proved to be a witty and ingenious Mr. Fix-It.

She remained in the shadows, waiting until Brody sauntered off. It had been a week since she'd told him she couldn't marry him because she couldn't give up the station. Even though he'd expressed some understanding and sympathy at the time, since then he'd been so distant. Not that she could blame him. In a strange way she was glad he didn't want to settle for an affair any more than she did.

Every day for a week now, she'd told herself it was better this way; that Brody was doing her a favor by keeping his distance; that now she could put all her energies into her work, and Skye, and helping her sisters plan her dad's upcoming marriage to Mellie.

She felt tears sting her eyes, thinking about her dad and Mellie's wedding. No, that wasn't it. What brought on the tears was thinking of the wedding that was never going to be: her wedding to Brody.

She clenched her jaw. This was nuts. She'd spent the last seven years adamant that she never wanted to get married again. Deep down, she'd always clung to that dumb agreement with Arnie about the station, because in part, anyway, she saw it as a means of protecting herself from making the same mistake twice. Now she had to ask herself, if she could renegotiate that deal with Arnie, and somehow retain ownership of the station—single *or* married—would she have said yes to Brody?

A pointless question, she concluded, since that wasn't going to happen.

"What did you think?"

The unexpected sound of Brody's voice made her jump. She thought he was still on the set, talking to Mr. Fix-It.

"I'm sorry," she muttered blankly, having heard his voice but not the words.

"The show. What did you think of the show?"

"Oh. Oh, great. It was really great. If I ever have to patch up a hole in my wall I'll know...just what to do."

An awkward silence set in. There didn't seem to be much to say to each other anymore, Kate thought sadly. She struggled for something. Something strictly to do with business. "So, how's the 'Comedy Club' lineup coming along? I hear you auditioned Carl's girlfriend, Cindy, the other day."

Brody smiled crookedly. "Oh, right, the dental hygienist." He leaned a little closer to her. "As the judge said to the dentist: Do you swear to pull the tooth, the whole tooth, and nothing but the tooth?"

Kate stared at Brody. Then all of a sudden she burst into laughter. "You think that's funny, huh?" Brody quipped. "Then you'd have been rolling on the floor laughing over some of her other jokes."

"No . . . it's . . . not funny. It's . . . awful," she said between spurts of girlish giggles. "It's even worse . . . than Carl's . . .umbrella joke."

Brody didn't join in on her laughter, but he was smiling at her with such tenderness that it brought her up short.

"What?" she asked, feeling exceedingly self-conscious and ridiculously pleased by that smile at the same time. It had been a while since she'd seen him smile at her. Seven long days. Seven lonely nights.

"The sound of your laughter," he said softly. "It's . . . nice," he finished lamely.

Her eyes met his. "I haven't felt much like laughing this past week."

"Neither have I," Brody confessed.

"Brody . . ."

"Kate . . ."

"You first," she said.

"I need some time off. I have some stuff to attend to. Back in San Francisco."

Kate's mouth went dry. "How . . . long?"

Brody shrugged. "I'm not sure."

"I see."

He scrutinized her expression. "What do you see?"

"Nothing. Just take as much . . . time as you need."

She started to turn away, but he caught her arm. "I'm talking a few days. Maybe a week."

"Fine."

"You don't believe me. You think I'm running out on you."

She pried his fingers from her arm. "Look, Brody, under the circumstances, maybe it's . . . just as well." She had to turn away from him or he'd see the misery etched all over her face.

Brody threw up his hands in frustration. "Kate, when will you ever get it in your head that I'm not Arnie or Oscar or whatever other jerk was stupid enough to leave you. I'm coming back."

She felt a spurt of tears fill her eyes and she was glad she wasn't facing him. "You don't get it. I want you to go. I think it would be best for both of us. And for Skye, too."

"Is that really what you think would be best, Katie?" He put his hands lightly on her shoulders, feeling her stiffen at his touch. He immediately lifted his hands away.

"It would never work out for us, Brody. I'm sorry." She thought she could hear her heart breaking, but she told herself that she had to make him believe it was over for her. What she couldn't figure out was, Why? Was it because she knew he never meant to come back, anyway? Or because she was afraid that otherwise he might come back?

He didn't answer for what felt like an eternity. Then, when he did, she wished eternity had lasted a little longer.

"I'm leaving first thing in the morning."

She didn't trust herself to speak so she just nodded. And then she walked out of the studio. *He's leaving. And he isn't coming back. I can hear it in his voice. I've lost him for good.* The words played over and over again in her mind....

"WHAT DO YOU MEAN he's gone?" Rachel demanded of Kate the next morning when Kate walked into her office at WPIT.

"He went back to San Francisco," Kate said, quite amazed at how calm her voice sounded when inwardly she felt as if she were dying. Surely, some part of her had died.

"Why? When's he coming back?"

"I don't know," Kate said, opening a report she needed to attend to that morning.

"Which don't you know?" Rachel demanded. "Why? Or when he's due back?"

"Both. He didn't tell me why. Or...when," Kate said, a little tremor creeping into her voice despite herself.

Julie popped into the office. "I just went down to talk to Brody about tonight's show and he isn't in yet."

Rachel gave her sister a meaningful look. "He's gone."

Julie scowled. "Gone where?"

"San Francisco," Rachel answered.

"Why? When's he...?"

"Please, Julie," Kate said, cutting her sister off sharply. "I have a lot of work to do. And so do both of you. Brody's gone. And I have no idea when he's coming back. Or even . . . if he's coming back. That's it. Now, could you both please . . ."

"You sent him," Julie said, her eyes narrowing. "You sent him off, didn't you, Kate?"

"No," she countered. "It was his decision. He told me right after the 'Mr. Fix-It' show yesterday that he needed to go back to San Francisco, and I said . . . fine."

"Fine?" Julie echoed. "All you said was fine?"

Rachel folded her hands across her chest. "And I bet you're real proud of yourself. Letting him go off without even a word about how you really feel, not a whisper about how desperately in love with him you are, how much you want him to stay."

"I don't want him to stay," Kate said stubbornly. "When he told me he was coming back, I told him . . . it would be best if he didn't. That there was no point . . ."

"Oh, you're so strong. So tough," Julie said.

"I have to be," Kate argued. Only her bottom lip was starting to tremble. She had to compress her lips tightly together.

"Damn it, Kate," Rachel said softly. "You don't have to be tough around us. Don't you think we know what you're going through?"

Kate's whole body started to shake. Suddenly, she dropped her head in her arms on her desk. She couldn't hold her feelings back anymore. "How am I going to live without him?" she moaned. "How am I ever going to stop wanting him?"

Julie and Rachel came up on either side of their sister. "Kate," Julie said. "Arnie's willing to sell you the station."

Kate's head popped up, tears streaming down her face. "What?"

"Unfortunately, we can't figure out a way to come up with enough money to swing it."

Kate shifted her gaze from Julie to Rachel. She didn't know what to say.

"The thing is," Rachel said, "we want you to know we weren't doing it for ourselves. And Julie and I both know that we're a big part of why you're determined to stay at the helm. Being at WPIT is great, Kate, but I've been thinking of leaving for some time now. Working and looking after one kid is hard enough. With another on the way, it's just going to be too much. I want to stay home until at least they're both in school."

"And as for Ben and me," Julie said, "we've been fielding offers from a lot of stations all across the country to do a talk show together. Not that we've ever griped about the money here, but heck, we could do better elsewhere."

"Face it, Kate. So could you and Brody," Rachel said. "You've both got incredible talent and experience. And there are tons of new cable stations popping up every day."

Tears ran down Kate's cheeks. She put an arm around each of her sisters and pulled them to her. "Do you two really think, after all these years, I can't see through you?"

They started to protest, but Kate cut them off.

"You don't want to leave this place any more than I do, so don't either of you even waste your breath denying it."

Julie gave her sister a level look. "Okay, but let me tell you something that's the absolute truth, Kate Hart. If I were in your place, I wouldn't give up the man I love for anything. And none of us—not me, Rachel here, Ben, Delaney, Dad—want to feel responsible for you having given up your one chance of true happiness for us. We're all grown up, Kate. We can take care of ourselves. It's time you stopped playing big sister."

"You're forgetting one very important person that isn't all grown up," Kate said. "Skye."

"She adores Brody," Rachel said.

"She deserves having a father," Julie added.

"She already has a father," Kate said. "And a home. Friends she's known her whole life. Family..."

"You ask yourself this, Kate," Rachel said. "Would Brody love Skye like his own? Would the three of you—you, Brody and Skye—be a family? No matter where you lived?"

Again, tears began running down Kate's cheeks in earnest. "It's... true." She felt a surge of panic sweep through her. "But it's too late. It's over. I sent him away. I told him not to come back."

Julie and Rachel tugged Kate to her feet. "Then what are you doing sitting around this moth-eaten place?" Julie said.

Rachel reached for the phone. She got Marcia over at Pittsville Travel on the second ring. Before Kate's tears had time to dry on her face she had a seat booked on a noon flight from Boston direct to San Francisco.

Delaney drove her to Logan airport in his police cruiser so that she wouldn't miss her flight.

"WOULD YOU LIKE A pillow or a magazine?"

Kate looked dully up at the flight attendant. It took a couple of moments for the trim, young uniformed woman's words to filter through the haze that had enveloped her head. "Oh, no. No, thanks. I'm . . . fine."

Fine? The last thing in the world she was, was fine. *What am I doing here? Why did I let them talk me into this?*

It had all happened so fast. One minute she was sobbing, the next she was being hustled into Delaney's cruiser, her suitcase tossed in the back seat. She hadn't even stopped at home to pack. Julie had seen to that. Heaven only knew what she'd thrown into the suitcase. And then she was at the airport, Delaney hurrying her through the terminal to her gate, giving her a kiss on the cheek, wishing her luck and shoving her in the direction of her plane.

So here she was. Flying over Nebraska or some such spot. What was she going to do when she landed? She wasn't even sure where in San Francisco Brody had gone. Or, for that matter, if he'd even gone to San Francisco. Maybe he'd changed his mind. Maybe he'd lied to her.

No. No, he hadn't lied. She was the one who'd run scared—not him.

Not that WPIT wasn't really important to her, but Julie and Rachel were right. It wasn't worth keeping if it meant losing the love of her life. She saw that now. They could all—including herself—manage without WPIT. They were all bright, resourceful, talented.

There were plenty of jobs out there. Love was something else altogether. Love didn't come along very often. Not the kind of love "ever after" that Skye had talked about. The kind of love her dad and Mellie shared, Julie and Ben, Rachel and Delaney. The kind of love she and Brody could have.

She shut her eyes. *I'm ready, Brody. I'm not scared anymore. I'm terrified, but I'm not scared.*

SOMEWHERE OVER NEVADA, Kate began to feel a little sick to her stomach. Nerves, she told herself. Nothing but nerves. Or maybe it was getting to be around that time of the month. She always lost track. *Now let me think. When exactly am I due?* She started to calculate....

"Oh," she yelped, sitting bolt upright in the chair. The man sitting beside her, a businessman type in a navy suit, looked over at her with alarm.

"Are you ill, miss?"

She stared at him. "No. Well, yes. No."

"You aren't sure?"

"No. Not absolutely sure." A smile lit up her face. "I think so, though. I feel..."

"Sick?"

Her smile deepened. "No. No, I feel wonderful. Absolutely wonderful."

A COUPLE OF HOURS LATER, as she stared at the pink strip of paper in the rest room of a San Francisco coffee shop, she still couldn't fully believe it. Maybe the test was wrong. Maybe if it turned pink it meant she wasn't pregnant. She checked the box again. Nope. Pink meant yes, all right.

Kate leaned against the stall, trying to sort out how she felt now that it was a reality. Even though she hadn't taken any precautions with Brody those two times they'd made love, she'd never really thought for a moment that she was taking any serious risk. Her tubes were clogged with scar tissue. When she got pregnant with Skye after three years of trying, the doctor had thought it close to a miracle. And after she'd delivered, he'd told her miracles rarely happened twice. Not that Kate had given up trying even though Arnie had told her one was enough and he didn't want any more. This from the man who had three children with his second wife.

As she stood in front of 1432 Poe Street, a quaint sky blue Victorian house with mint green gingerbread trim, the address she'd gotten off Brody's résumé, Kate felt incredibly nervous, her initial high spirits having taken a distinct nosedive. What would she say to Brody? Would he think the only reason she'd come, the only reason she'd decided to accept his proposal, was that she was pregnant with his child? Should she tell him right off? What if he'd changed his mind? What if he no longer wanted to marry her? Maybe her send-off had been the last straw for him.

Kate literally jumped as the front door of the house opened and a beautiful, willowy young woman with flowing blond hair and an absolutely exquisite toddler in her arms appeared in the doorway. "Hi. I saw you standing out there and wondered if you were lost or something."

A vision of the past assaulted Kate. Oscar Foote's wife and child at her front door. *Oh, God,* she thought as her eyes fell on the woman and child at this door. *Please don't let this be happening to me again!*

Kate numbly shook her head. "No. I was looking for... Is this where Brody Baker lives? I mean, where he used to live? That is, he wouldn't be here by any chance?"

"Afraid you just missed him. I'm Anne Brody. Can I help you?"

"Anne? You mean... Annie?"

The young woman laughed. "Only my big brother calls me Annie."

Kate laughed, too. A giddy laugh. "I'm Kate. Only your big brother calls me Katie."

"Katie? Oh my God."

"You... know who I am?"

"Know who you are? My brother was here for an hour and your name must have come up at least a hundred times. What are you doing here?" Anne exclaimed.

"Good question," Kate said. "I'm not really sure." She paused for a moment, then she smiled from ear to ear. "That's not true. I am sure."

Annie grinned. "Well, then, you'd better come inside."

BOTH WOMEN GIGGLED like schoolgirls when Brody walked into the living room of his former abode and did a classic double take at the sight of Kate sitting cross-legged on the floor, bouncing his eighteen-month-old nephew on her lap.

"Hi," she said cheerily, as if it were the most natural thing in the world that she'd be there.

Brody, dazed, slumped down on the closest chair. "I'm seeing things, right?"

"I'll tell you that after you tell me whether you like what you see," Kate replied.

"Hold it," Annie said, scooping up her son, Brian, from Kate and taking hold of her four-year-old Lucy's hand. "Exit extras."

"I wanna color with Uncle Brody," Lucy protested.

"Later, Lucy. Later," Annie said, ushering her brood out of the room.

"Well?" Kate asked.

Brody stared at her in silence for such a long time that Kate began to panic.

"I didn't mean what I said yesterday, Brody. I guess I was so sure you were going for good, I was just making it easier for you."

"I left my Harley parked in your driveway. I thought that would give you a clue that I'd be back."

"I . . . didn't know. I wasn't home." Her eyes widened. No, she hadn't been home. But Julie had. Julie had dashed back there to pack her suitcase. Julie had to have seen the bike, had to have known he'd be coming back. There was no reason for her to have flown clear across the country like a mad hatter. He was coming back.

"She didn't say a word," Kate muttered.

"Who?"

She started to tell him who, but changed her mind. "It doesn't matter. I came out here because there's something I didn't tell you before you left."

"Must be something important."

"It is."

"Well, I have something important to tell you, too."

"You do?" she asked expectantly.

"You first."

She stared at him. She was still sitting on the floor in the middle of the living room and Brody remained in his chair near the entrance about ten feet away. She rose, but she didn't move any closer. She just stood there, her arms dangling at her sides. "What I flew out here to tell you is . . . I love you, Brody." Absently, her hand went to her stomach. "I don't want to have to choose between you and WPIT, but since I do have to choose, I choose you, Brody." She exhaled a breath. "I guess . . . that's it." Well, not quite, but it was enough for starters. "Now you."

"Wait. I want to be sure I'm hearing right. You choose me over the station?"

She nodded.

"Meaning you'd marry me, even though it means—"

"Yes, that's what I mean. I want to marry you, Brody Baker, more than I've ever wanted anything in my whole life." She hesitated. "Except for maybe one other thing."

Brody slowly got to his feet. "And what's that?"

A timorous smile played on her lips. "Another baby. I've always dreamed of having another baby."

Brody closed the distance between them in two long strides. He wrapped Kate in his arms. "If that's what you want, Katie, that's what you'll get. I promise you. I'll make that dream come true."

She touched his cheek very gently, then looked him square in the face. This was it. "You already have, Brody."

"I don't . . ."

"I'm . . . pregnant."

"You're . . . what?"

"As in, I'm going to have a baby. Our baby. I felt something on the plane flying over here. Isn't that crazy? I felt this funny, queasy feeling in my stomach and at first I thought . . . But then, it hit me. I was sure even before I took the test."

"You took a . . . test?"

"A pregnancy test. After we landed I rushed to the nearest drugstore and bought one of those kits. Brody, I want you to know I decided to marry you before I knew. I'm not marrying you because I'm pregnant. I want this baby. I want it no matter what. So, you don't have to marry me. If you've changed your mind . . ."

Brody swayed a little. "I need to sit down. I'm feeling kind of light-headed."

Kate laughed as she guided him over to the sofa. "Hey, I'm the one that's pregnant."

Brody's expression instantly filled with concern. "Are you okay? Are you dizzy or sick?"

"No. I feel fine."

"You're really pregnant?"

"You want to see the pink slip?"

Brody gave her a puzzled look.

She grinned. "Never mind. Yes, Brody. I'm really pregnant. You might say it's a miracle."

He drew her into his arms. "You might say? Oh, no, heart of my heart, it is a miracle. The most wonderful miracle in the world. Our baby." He pulled back to look at her. "Say, does Skye know?"

"How could she? I only figured it out—"

"Let's call her. Let's call everyone. No, wait. I have a better idea. Let's go home, Katie."

She smiled wistfully. "Home for a little while, anyway. Until we get married. You *are* going to marry me, Brody Baker?"

"Kate, I'm going to marry you and we're going to settle down to a wonderful life together in Pittsville."

"I don't understand."

Brody pulled a bank check from his leather jacket pocket. He held it up to Kate.

Her eyes were wide as saucers as she stared at the amount of money the check was made out for. And they got even wider when she saw whom the check was made out to—Arnold Pilcher.

"What . . . ?"

"We're buying the station, Kate. Arnie's lawyers are drawing up the papers as we speak."

"But where did you get all this money?"

He wagged a finger at her. "Well, I didn't rob a bank for it, if that's what's worrying you. Believe me, my jailhouse days are long behind me."

"Then how?"

"Oil, Katie. My daddy invested in oil back in Texas in the days when oil was king. And he got out before it all ran dry. Set up tidy trust funds for me and Annie. Truth is, I've never dipped into mine till now. Never felt a need. Never wanted anything all that badly. Oh, but Katie," he murmured, pulling her back into his arms, "I want *you* that badly."

"And I wanted you badly enough to give it up."

He smiled lovingly. "I know. That's something I'm never going to forget."

Epilogue

December 25

Well, all I can say is Santa sure gave me what I wanted for Christmas. A new stepdad. And a very special added bonus—a new baby sister or brother on the way.

And the wedding. It's one Pittsville will long remember, that's for sure. Certainly one our family won't forget. I mean, how many couples invite thousands of guests to their wedding?

Yep. Brody and Mom got married on TV this very afternoon. On WPIT's newest show on the winter lineup, to be exact—"Wedding Belles." Today was the premiere. Bet the show gets the highest ratings ever. Naturally, it was Brody's idea. Television weddings. One a month. We've already got the show booked through June. Grandpa Leo and Mellie have the June date.

The wedding was totally awesome. I got to be Mom's maid of honor and I wore this real neat dark blue velvet dress and my very first pair of heels. They were satin and matched my dress. Okay, my feet killed me, but the pain was worth it.

Gee, it was just one major excitement after another. Mom said if I wanted, I could invite a boy to the wedding. She didn't exactly say a "date." Of course, both she and Brody knew who I wanted to ask. I was a nervous wreck about doing it, though. It was Brody who helped give me the courage. I almost died when Robby said yes. Not just "Yes." He said he'd "love to come." (He and Alice broke up before Thanksgiving, so it wasn't like I was trying to break them up or anything. She wasn't at all upset that he was with me. She brought this new boy, Josh, to the wedding. So we were all happy. Robby and I danced four slow dances.)

Even though the ceremony was in the studio, it really was almost like being in church, thanks to the great job of decorating and set building that was supervised by Aunt Julie and Aunt Rachel. Pastor Morgan presided under a canopy of flowers. Tulips, naturally. Meg played the "Wedding March" and Gus turned the pages for her. It wouldn't surprise me if they make it on the show one of these months.

After the service, we had a big party at the station for all our friends and family. The food was great—even the strange concoctions Meg contributed. Next week she's going to do a "wedding dinner" meal for her cooking show, so she's happy as blueberry pie. The blueberry pie, compliments of the Full Moon, I should add, was super.

One of the best parts of the day was that I got to meet my new Aunt Annie and Uncle Paul and their adorable kids. Lucy was the flower girl and she looked like an angel in white organdy. Annie was totally neat, and she invited me out to stay with them in San Francisco this summer. Mom said sure.

And speaking of Mom . . . Wow, I always knew she was really pretty and all, but, like, she's my mom, right? And moms are . . .well, moms. Only today, she wasn't just a mom. She was this fairy princess, dressed in this long, flowing, pale blue satin gown, with a silver crown and lacy veil. Really, she did look like she'd just stepped out of a fairy tale. She was *beautiful.* And Brody was part of a fairy tale, too. Prince Charming in a black tuxedo with a red satin cummerbund and a red bow tie. And of course, his boots! Mom insisted.

Hey, is this funny, or what? I just realized I've come to the very last page of my journal. As Grandpa Leo would say, all's well that ends well.

This month's
irresistible novels from

HEART TO HEART by Elise Title

Third in *The Hart Girls* trilogy

Kate Hart had had too many run-ins with Mr. Wrong and she would be darned if she would let Brody Baker smooth-talk his way into her heart...and into her bed. No matter *how* sexy he was!

THE TROUBLE WITH BABIES by Madeline Harper

Cal Markam was Annie Valentine's toughest case. She was hired to mould the millionaire playboy into a conservative company president, but a rumour was circulating that he had fathered twins! A man like Cal could only mean trouble. Double trouble.

SERVICE WITH A SMILE by Carolyn Andrews

Sunny Caldwell was determined to succeed and had two golden rules—to put her personal delivery service first and never to get involved with a client. She followed her rules until the day she met Chase Monroe and his needy family.

PLAIN JANE'S MAN by Kristine Rolofson

Plain Jane won a man. Well, not exactly. Feisty and independent Jane Plainfield won a boat. The man, gorgeous boat designer Peter Johnson, just seemed to come with it!

Spoil yourself next month
with these four novels from

Temptation

IN PRAISE OF YOUNGER MEN by Lyn Ellis

Will Case was too big, far too attractive and much, much too sexy. And for the next few months, he would be sharing a cabin with Carolina. Will was also best friends with her little brother—and the same age!

THE RELUCTANT HUNK by Lorna Michaels

Ariel Foster wanted Jeff McBride to do a series for her TV station. She knew every woman in town would tune in to watch the drop-dead gorgeous man, if only she could persuade him to work for her. But she soon realised she wanted the reluctant hunk for herself.

BACHELOR HUSBAND by Kate Hoffmann

Come live and love in L.A. with the tenants of Bachelors Arms. The first in a captivating new mini-series.

Tru Hallihan lives in this trendy apartment block and has no thoughts of settling down. But he can't resist a bet to date popular radio presenter, Caroline Leighton. Caroline will only co-operate at a price—Tru must pose as her husband for a day!

SECOND-HAND BRIDE by Roseanne Williams

Brynn had married Flint Wilder knowing he was on the rebound from her twin sister, Laurel. Six months later, Brynn had left Flint, fearing she'd never be more than a substitute for her twin. Now Brynn was back in town and Flint seemed hell-bent on making up. But could she ever be sure she wasn't just a stand-in for her sister?